MW00941944

Secrets on the Sand

The Barefoot Bay Series #1

roxanne st. claire

Cover art by Robin Ludwig Design Inc.
Interior formatting by Author E.M.S.
Seashell graphic used with permission under Creative Commons CC0 public domain.

ISBN-13: 978-1500359829
ISBN-10: 1500359823

Published in the United States of America.

Critical Reviews of Roxanne St. Claire Novels

"St. Claire, as always, brings a scorching tear-up-the-sheets romance combined with a great story: dealing with real issues starring memorable characters in vivid scenes."
— *Romantic Times Magazine*

"Non-stop action, sweet and sexy romance, lively characters, and a celebration of family and forgiveness."
— *Publishers Weekly*

"Plenty of heat, humor, and heart!"
— *USA Today's Happy Ever After blog*

"It's safe to say I will try any novel with St. Claire's name on it."
— *www.smartbitchestrashybooks.com*

"The writing was perfectly on point as always and the pace of the story was flawless. But be forewarned that you will laugh, cry, and sigh with happiness. I sure did."
— *www.harlequinjunkies.com*

"The Barefoot Bay series is an all-around knockout, soul-satisfying read. Roxanne St. Claire writes with warmth and heart and the community she's built at Barefoot Bay is one I want to visit again and again."
— *Mariah Stewart, New York Times bestselling author*

"This book stayed with me long after I put it down."
— *All About Romance*

The Barefoot Bay Series

Welcome to Barefoot Bay! On these sun-washed shores you'll meet heroes who'll steal your heart, heroines who'll make you stand up and cheer, and characters who quickly become familiar and beloved. Some are spicy, some are sweet, but every book in the Barefoot Bay series stands alone, and tempts readers to come back again and again. So, kick off your shoes and fall in love with billionaires, brides, bodyguards, silver foxes, and more...all on one dreamy island.

THE BAREFOOT BAY SERIES

Want to know the day the next Roxanne St. Claire book is released? Sign up for the newsletter! You'll get brief monthly e-mails about new releases and book sales.

http://www.roxannestclaire.com/newsletter.html

Secrets on the Sand

roxanne st. claire

Dedication

*This title is dedicated to reader, friend and fan
Tonya Loose Dawson in appreciation for
her constant support and cheerleading!*

Chapter One

"**O**h, how the mighty have fallen."

Amanda froze at the sound of Tori Drake's sneer, refusing to react even though the cold porcelain of the toilet rim pressed against her forearm as she brushed the bowl.

"Mandy Mitchell's up to her elbows in someone else's shit."

Of all the other housekeepers to be assigned to the same floor, she had to get Tori. "As you know, I go by Amanda Lockhart now."

"Ah, you'll always be Mandy Mitchell to me, hon. Homecoming queen. Head cheerleader. Runner-up for Miss Teen Florida. Junior housekeeper." She choked softly. "What's wrong with this résumé, kids?"

Breathing slowly, holding it together, Amanda sat straight, the move pressing the hard tile into her knees with the same force that Tori's insults hit her heart. But not as much force as she'd like her fist to hit the other housekeeper's face.

"Do you need anything to finish your rooms?" Amanda asked, faking nice as much as she possibly could. She was too far behind this morning to get into it with Tori. Besides, if the universe decided it hated Amanda enough, she could very well be calling this woman "boss" soon. The thought made her almost want to hurl into the toilet instead of clean it.

"Oh, I don't need a thing," Tori said.

"You sure? Because my supply cart is right there, and I've got plenty of Pine-Sol and Clorox." *In case you want to drink a little.*

"Nah, I've cleaned all my rooms, of course. That's why they call me the fastest maid in Barefoot Bay. Possibly on all of the Gulf Coast. Maybe the entire state of Florida."

"Why not the world?"

"Why not?" Tori snorted with self-satisfaction and stepped further into the bathroom, which was sizable, being in a high-end resort hotel, but no room was big enough for the two of them. Uninvited, Tori leaned lazily on the granite vanity, sliding a judgmental finger over the surface. "You didn't use the Magic Eraser on this."

"I'm not done yet."

"Oh, you're just about done, my friend."

At the smug tone and the subtle warning, Amanda twisted from the toilet to look up at the other housekeeper, narrowing her eyes. "What does that mean?"

Tori crossed arms well-toned from hard work and deeply tanned from years of baby-oil-and-iodine-infused sunbathing. Her gray eyes danced with a secret, and derision pulled at her lips. "We are very close to a done deal."

Amanda's heart dropped. This was the worst possible news. "I'll believe it when I see it," she said.

Tori arched a penciled brow, forming lines on her forehead. More lines than Amanda had, considering they were the same age of thirty. The thought gave Amanda small consolation since beauty and lines now took a back seat to money and survival.

"Then you better believe it, sister." Tori pushed her butt onto the counter. "My man Jared has nearly closed financing and has made an offer on office space right in downtown Mimosa Key, not ten minutes down the beach. J&T Housekeeping, LLC, is about to be a reality, and guess what that means?"

The end of the world. Well, not quite. But most likely the end of this job. Once Casa Blanca Resort & Spa outsourced housekeeping to one company, then Amanda would have to work for that company or leave the resort. If "J&T Housekeeping" got the business... unemployment loomed.

"It means congratulations are in order," Amanda said, barely keeping the bitter out of her voice. But it was hard not to be bitter. Amanda had made the huge mistake of nursing the fantasy of opening that housekeeping firm herself when resort management announced the outsourcing plan. The taste of independence, of owning a business, of never having to clean a toilet again, had been sweet...for about two weeks.

She'd even met with the resort owner to talk about it. Then she'd done enough research to learn that the venture would require about five grand in starting capital. Which would be about $4,900 more than Amanda had to her name.

"You bet congrats are in order." Tori crossed her ankles and swung her feet. "The first thing Jared's going to do is put me in the office and out of other people's toilets."

Envy wormed its ugly way up Amanda's chest, even though she knew that jealousy was exactly what Tori wanted.

"What will *you* do?" Tori asked, as if they didn't both know that the first order of "office" business would be to fire Amanda. Or give her the worst shifts imaginable. "I mean, what are you trained to do? Not too many beauty contest options around these days. Maybe you could go coach the cheering staff down at Mimosa High. Still have your old uniform, Mandy the Magnificent?"

Oh, Tori loved to pull out that old high school nickname, didn't she? "I have to work," Amanda said.

"You sure do. And that's a stunner for you, isn't it? Thought you'd be some rich guy's wife and give parties and have tea. But that didn't work out for you so well, did it?"

No, it hadn't worked out at all. She stabbed the toilet brush harder, biting back a response.

In Tori's pocket, her cell buzzed, offering a reprieve. She pulled it out and read a text. "Oh, boy. That guy who checked into Bay Laurel yesterday is going out for lunch and wants the villa cleaned ASAP."

Amanda looked up. "I'm not scheduled to do any of the villas until after three o'clock today."

Tori lifted a tough-shit shoulder. "Sucks to suck."

"I can't—"

"Hey, hey, hey." She waved a warning finger back and forth. "You know the company motto. Can't is a four-letter word at Casa Blanca Resort & Spa."

Amanda had heard Lacey and Clay Walker, the resort owners, make the statement enough times at all-staff meetings that she swallowed her argument.

"Anyway." Tori pushed off the counter and slapped

her work sneakers on the floor. "Management's watching. Dude's some kind of big-ass deal, and they are giving him the royal treatment. You better get over there and clean your sweet cheeks off, babycakes."

"Me?" She sputtered the syllable. "I've got three more rooms to do here in the hotel before I can start the villas. These have to be done before noon."

Tori smoothed her uniform, the same peach and brown as Amanda's, but much tighter. "Sorry, darling, I have a date with Jared for lunch." She gave an evil grin. "Business planning and then...my reward for getting my work done early." She turned to smooth stick-straight blonde hair in the mirror.

There was no way Amanda could clean that villa *and* finish this floor by noon. "Come on, Tori. It's one guy in a huge villa. Can't you run over there and do a quick job before you go to lunch? Or maybe pick up one of my rooms?"

Tori never looked away from the mirror, dabbing at her mascara. "You know what your problem is, Mandy?"

She had a feeling she was about to find out.

"You're not driven enough. You think you can get by on your good looks, but, honey girl, have you *looked* at yourself lately?" She turned from the mirror to stare down at Amanda, tsking softly. "It's like you forgot who you once were." Very slowly, Tori crouched down, getting face to face with her. "But the rest of the nothings and nobodies in your royal court haven't forgotten a thing."

Despite the assault of sour breath and mean spirit, Amanda refused to cower. "You better go, Tori. Jared's waiting. It's time for you and your husband...oh, I mean fiancé. Oh, wait." She couldn't resist. "He hasn't given you a ring yet, has he?"

Tori stood quickly. "At least I didn't get dumped and end up living with my parents. And, oh, I'm not four rooms behind on my morning work." She lifted her foot and tapped the side of the toilet with her sneaker's toe. "You missed a spot, angel."

The fastest way to the beachfront villas was via a golf cart up the stone walkway that led from the main resort through the entire Casa Blanca property, but, of course, no carts were available when Amanda needed one. She didn't relish walking the path, but not because of the hot sun or tropical heat. In January, the Florida barrier island's humidity was tempered with lovely Gulf breezes, and the view of Barefoot Bay usually lifted her mood. But walking the path generally meant rubbing elbows with the well-heeled resort guests, as they meandered from the exclusive villas to the private beach.

Not so long ago, Amanda had at least felt at home with the beautiful people strolling through resorts like this one, wondering which four-hundred-dollar cover-up to wear to the beach or whether she should have champagne or chilled vodka after her oxygen facial. Now? She couldn't remember the last time she tasted champagne or did more than wash her face before falling into bed, bone-tired from cleaning toilets and scrubbing showers.

Honey girl, have you looked *at yourself lately?*

Tori's words stung, even though Amanda didn't need to worry about how she looked. She needed to worry about how to pay debts on a maid's income without depending on…on *anyone*. Amanda Lockhart would never again depend on a man, a friend, a parent, or a gift.

Shouldering the weight of a bucket full of supplies in one hand and a long work mop in the other, she held on to that unwavering objective. To erase the ugly conversation she'd had with Tori, she peered through palm fronds and over sea oats to the turquoise Gulf of Mexico sparkling in the sun. But even the splash of yellow beach umbrellas and the squawks of seagulls and terns didn't cheer her.

If J&T Housekeeping became a reality and got the business to provide all of the cleaning services for this small but upscale resort, she'd have to leave this slice of paradise. And she'd have to find something to do for work, because she wasn't going to be able to stay at her parents' house much longer. Their round-the-country RV adventure would be ending soon, and she wasn't going to live with them. It was too humiliating and suffocating.

Although, she should have been used to humiliation and suffocation. Doug Lockhart had been quite adept at putting her through both.

She arrived at the two-story vacation villa only slightly damp and out of breath. Setting her bucket down, but still holding the mop, she pulled out her master card key from the lanyard around her neck and tapped on the mahogany door.

"Housekeeping!" she called automatically before sliding the key in the lock.

She waited a beat, then tapped again and started to turn the knob, but the door whipped open from the other side, practically yanking her arm with it.

"You're here now?" A man loomed in silhouette, backlit from the patio well behind him.

"You asked for…" She blinked as he took a step closer and she could see him clearly, losing her train of thought as she met Gulf-blue eyes fringed with dark lashes. Straight ebony hair brushed the collar of an expensive shirt. He was all black and blue…which was probably the shape this man left every heart he encountered. "I'm here to clean."

But he seemed speechless, too, holding her gaze for a heartbeat or two, a frown pulling at his thick brows as he studied her—hard—then glanced at her mop. "I see that." His eyes back on her face again, he searched every inch, from brow to chin and back again.

The scrutiny lasted one second too long, so she lifted the card key, flipping it to show her ID. "I'm with the resort." Because he looked like he didn't believe her. Or at least he didn't believe…something. "You asked for your villa to be cleaned?"

"Uh, yeah, but later."

Damn it! Tori had lied to her to throw off her schedule. Now she'd have to trudge all the way back down to the hotel. "All right, sorry for the incon—"

"No, wait." He almost reached for her, then caught himself. "Stay and…clean." He nearly swallowed the last word, as if it didn't sound right to him.

"I don't have—"

"Who are you?" he asked, still staring at her face.

Oh, jeez. Just her luck to get the nutcase. Great-looking, but a guest didn't care what the maid's name

8

was unless he had a screw loose.

"I'm Amanda Lockhart from housekeeping." She bent to scoop up the bucket as if that could prove it. "I was informed the Bay Laurel villa was ready for cleaning, but I can come back at a better time."

"No, it's just that…" His voice trailed off. Easily six-two with broad shoulders in a crisp white shirt tucked into pleated khaki pants, he wasn't simply gorgeous, he oozed that indefinable something that came with money, class, and power. On most men, that revolted her. On him? Had to admit, nothing was revolting. "I have a guest," he finally said.

She stepped back quickly, imagining some sultry brunette stripping down in his bedroom. Maybe two of them, by the looks of this guy. "I'll come back. Say, three o'clock?"

Laser-blue eyes sliced her. "Do I know you?" His voice was tinged with something she couldn't pinpoint in that split second. Hope? Expectation? *Something*.

"Doubtful." She croaked the word, probably because there was no way anyone who had a single female hormone floating in her bloodstream would forget him. "Sorry to bother you, sir."

"No," he said quickly, opening the door even wider. "No, please. Come in…" That frown pulled again. "Amanda, did you say?"

She hesitated a second longer. "Not if you're in the middle of something with a…a friend."

The hint of a smile pulled at full lips, his eyes crinkling with a flicker of humor. "Not a friend." He leaned a little closer and whispered, "But if I tell you who it is, you have to promise not to laugh."

She didn't move, her senses slammed by a clean,

masculine scent and the low timbre of secret in his voice.

"It's my mother," he said, the smile widening. "And if you're not careful, she'll want to help you clean."

She let out a quick laugh, the nerves receding but not the toe-curling impact of him. "I don't need any help, but if you're entertaining…"

"I'm afraid she's not. Entertaining, that is." He backed up to clear the doorway for her. "We're on the patio."

With a little uncertainty, she stepped into the cool air and rich comfort of the Moroccan-inspired decor. He fit in a place like this, as though the high-end designer had planned the dark wood and plush furnishings around someone with his size and command.

Deep inside, a familiar warning bell rang with a reminder that she'd sworn off men. All men in general. This kind of man in particular. Especially one who continued to look at her too intensely.

"Why don't I start upstairs so I can stay out of your way?" Without waiting for a response, she walked toward the wrought iron banister, gripping her bucket and mop so they didn't slip out of damp palms. Still, she could feel him looking at her, those gas-flame blues burning a hole in her back. Tensing, she put one foot on a step before sneaking a peek over her shoulder.

Sure enough, he was staring. With so much intensity it stole her breath.

"Is something wrong?" she asked.

"I…I have the strangest question," he said, coming closer.

"Yes?" She braced herself for whatever it might be. A cleaning suggestion? A proposition? Maybe something as innocent as his favorite beer in the fridge? Guests could be strange. Not usually this drop-dead delicious, but strange.

He let out a self-conscious chuckle, shaking his head, a little color rising. Good heavens, was he *nervous*? Did this tall, dark, imposing master of the universe even know what insecurity was?

"Are you..." He angled his head, frowning hard, looking almost apologetic. "Are you Mandy Mitchell?"

Oh. Her knees buckled a little. Maybe with relief, maybe with that same shame that threatened her when Tori taunted with "senior adjectives" ripped from the pages of a yearbook.

"Not anymore," she said softly, the weight of the bucket becoming too much at that moment. As she set it on the step, she nodded with resignation. "But, yes, I was. Do I know you?" Because, whoa and damn, how was it possible she didn't remember meeting him?

"It is you." He broke into a slow, glorious smile that was like someone had switched on a spotlight, blinding and white, that softened the sharp angles of his face and shadow of whiskers in hollow cheeks.

"Zeke Nicholas." He took a few steps closer, reaching out his hand. "Mimosa High? Class of '02?"

She'd gone to high school with this guy? And hadn't dated him? Impossible. Without thinking, she lifted her free hand to his, getting another shock to the system when his fingers closed over hers, large and warm and strong and...tender. "I'm sorry...Zeke." *Zeke*? She'd never met a man with that name.

"Don't be sorry," he said, reluctantly releasing her hand. "We didn't exactly run in the same circles."

And why the heck not? "Are you sure?"

He laughed, the rumble in his chest a little too hearty

and sincere. "Yes, I'm sure."

"I'm sorry, I don't remember…" Anyone or anything that looked like him. "A Zeke."

"I went by my full name then." He gave her the most endearing smile that reached right into her chest and twisted her heart. "You're going to make me say it, aren't you?"

"To help me out?"

He looked down for a split second, then back to her face, the gesture shockingly humble for a man who couldn't be too familiar with humility. "Ezekiel Nicholas."

Her jaw dropped as a memory snapped into place. "Ezekiel the Geekiel?" The second she said it, she gasped softly and lifted her hands to her mouth. "I'm sorry." God, she was as bad as Tori throwing kids' nicknames around.

"No, no." He turned his hands up in surrender. "Guilty as charged by the dreaded senior adjectives." Then he leaned a little closer and lowered his voice, his face close enough for her to count individual lashes. "Mandy the Magnificent."

This time the words didn't sound ugly, spiteful, or laden with jealousy. On his lips, the words were a sexy, sweet whisper of admiration that made every nerve in her body dance.

Ezekiel Nicholas. How was this possible? How had that nerdy, skinny, four-eyed freak who could do Einstein-level math but couldn't make eye contact with a classmate turned into…a god?

"You've changed," she managed.

"You haven't." There was a softness to the words that nearly did her in, especially coming as an echo to the ones that had haunted her on the way up here.

Honey girl, have you looked *at yourself lately*?

Certainly not the way he was looking at her right now. A slow flush rose up from her chest and probably gave her cheeks some much-needed color. "Yes, I have changed," she said simply. "But clearly the years have been good to you."

"You work here." It was a statement of painful fact, but not the way he said it. "That's great." He actually sounded like he meant that, unlike others, who couldn't hide their amusement at the irony of Mandy Mitchell's fall from magnificent to maid. "Really, that's great."

"And you're staying here," she said after an uncomfortable few seconds passed. "With…your family?" He did say his mother was on the patio. Was there a Mrs. Nicholas? A Zeke Junior?

"I'm alone. My parents still live in the same house off Harbor Avenue, but I came back for a surprise party for my dad, so I decided to stay here."

For a long, awkward beat, they looked at each other through completely different eyes than the ones that met five minutes ago. Now, they had a history—or at least a shared past.

"Yeah, wow, Mandy." He shifted from one foot to the other, still kind of shaking his head like he couldn't believe what he was looking at. And who could blame him? She was a maid. He was a guy who rented thousand-dollar-a-night villas when he came to his hometown.

"Well, I…" She gestured toward the stairs. "I better get to work."

He gave her a slow smile, the kind that took long enough for a woman's heart to rise to her throat and fall to her feet.

"I'll be here for a week," he said.

"Oh, really?" Great, she'd have to see him every damn day. Him in his custom shirt over granite muscles and she in her housekeeping uniform and mop.

"Yeah, I was able to combine this trip with some business on the mainland, so…"

So…what? She nodded, unsure if she could simply walk away. Not that he was magnetic or anything. It would have been rude. And, dang, he *was* magnetic.

"Any chance we can get together?" he asked.

Was he asking her on a date? "Oh, I don't…" *Date. Ever. Remember, Amanda? Ever.* "I don't know…"

His gaze dropped over her uniform, lingering on the lanyard hanging around her neck, zeroing in on her name. "Oh, of course, you work here. Sorry." And no doubt her last name made him assume she was married.

"Yes, I work here," she said, hoping that would be enough excuse and explanation.

"Ezekiel?" A woman's voice interrupted Amanda, calling loudly from the patio. "I've got another one! Susan Fox confirmed for her and Jennifer. You remember Jennifer Fox, right? Really lovely and still single." Her voice rose with the last word, and Zeke looked skyward with an eye roll of complete frustration.

"'Kay," he called back. "Be right there." He leaned on the newel of the banister. "My mother is on a mission."

"Then you better go help her."

He puffed out a breath. "She doesn't need help, trust me. But…" He seemed entirely reluctant to move. "It's nice to see you," he finally said. "I always remembered you, Mandy."

She couldn't return the sentiment because, to be fair, she hadn't thought about Ezekiel Nicholas since... No, she'd never actually given him a moment's consideration. Ever. Until now, when she absolutely couldn't and shouldn't give him anything.

"I haven't been Mandy Mitchell for a long, long time," she said. That woman had died years ago, stomped out by a man not entirely unlike the one in front of her. "And, you know, judging from how I must have treated people in high school..." People like him. "That's probably a good thing."

His blue eyes widened in surprise. "How you treated people?"

"I was, you know, probably a little bit of an entitled bitch, but..." She made a self-deprecating gesture to her supplies. "What do they say? What goes around comes around?"

He gave her a look of sheer incredulity. "You weren't a bitch. You were beautiful."

The words nearly melted her. She opened her mouth to reply, but he lifted a hand and brushed his knuckles against her cheek. She almost shivered with the bolt of electricity that shot through her.

"Still are," he said softly.

"Ezekiel!"

Her throat closed too much to even dream of saying a word as he walked away. Silently, she trudged up the stairs, a mop in one hand, a bucket in the other, and the most unwanted longing pressing on her heart.

Ezekiel Nicholas was a dream, but he'd never be hers. She'd learned the hard way that dream men brought nightmares.

Chapter Two

It took Zeke a minute to force his teenage pathetic self back into the hole where he'd shoved him somewhere between MIT and Harvard Business School. He took slow steps to the open French doors, still processing what had just happened.

Since Zeke had been living in New York and amassing his wealth through hedge funds, Ezekiel the Geekiel had rarely emerged. Zeke often forgot that deep inside him lived a kid who squirmed at the thought of eye contact with any girl and turned positively pitiable when breathing the same air as Mandy Mitchell.

Who now worked as…a maid? What the hell was that all about?

Didn't matter what she was, because some things never changed. Holy hell, he was thirty years old, had a net worth that a small country would envy, and made speculative investments before his morning coffee that were so risky that failure meant professional—or real—suicide.

And then he morphed into a fucking schoolboy at the sight of an angel who'd once picked up his whole spilled backpack after some idiot tried to plow him down in the hall. That day freshman year, when he'd finally managed to look at her and choke out his awkward thanks, she'd smiled, and the sun came out and birds chirped and he fell head over heels in love.

He'd forgotten her, of course, over the years. But seeing her today brought back so many old feelings, he—

"Ezekiel, what is taking you so long?" On the pool patio, Mom stood with one hand on a narrow hip, tapping a cell phone impatiently against her cheek. She used the phone to point to the lists, notes, and papers she'd spread over the patio dining table. "I can't plan this whole event alone. I need your help."

"You're doing fine, Mom." He attempted to focus on his mother and her issues, not the housekeeper and her...grass-green eyes. "And the event's planned."

"We still have to round out the final table arrangements," she said. "And I'm having some good luck getting more young ladies to attend." She leaned to the side to peek around him through the French doors. She wore her sixty-eight years well, he had to admit, keeping trim and making sure not a single gray hair showed among the black. Her forehead crinkled mightily when she raised her brows in question. "Who were you talking to?"

"Just..." A memory. "The maid."

Why was she a housekeeper? The incongruity of that hit him like a two-by-four.

"Well, you didn't have to give her your life history."

He bit back a laugh at the irony of the statement. For a time, Mandy *was* his life history. At least, she was the object of a boyhood crush that had sure come crashing back at the sight of her. "I was giving her instructions."

"Why do you need a maid when you've barely slept in this place for one night? And so big, Ezekiel. Why do you need all this space?" She waved the phone at the villa, her dark eyes leveled at him in accusation. "Why spend all this money?"

"Because I have it."

"Pfft." She blew out a breath. "Money isn't everything, young man."

"Tell me about it." It sure hadn't impressed Mandy Mitchell enough to say yes to a date.

Okay, she had a different last name and so she was married. He had to give points to her for not taking his offer anyway, like plenty of women who could have rationalized a drink with an old high school classmate. Still, the rejection stung.

His mother was looking at him with so much pity, he could have sworn she was reading his mind. And with Violet Nicholas, the world's most intuitive mother, that was entirely possible.

"Oh, honey," she said, coming around the table to reach for him. "You see? I'm right. You're miserable."

He had to laugh. "I'm not miserable." At least he hadn't been until ten minutes ago. Would it have been so hard to have a drink with him? Okay, married, definitely. But he hadn't seen a ring.

"But are you happy?"

Happy? How should he answer that? Honestly, of course, and not only because he and his brother had decided years ago that Mom had "liedar." Her secret superpower had made an über-honest man out of him, which was both a blessing and a curse.

"I'm quite satisfied with my life," he said, adept at giving her a non-answer. And that wasn't a lie. He *was* satisfied. Like he was satisfied with a good massage, or a great haircut, or even some mindless sex.

Satisfied wasn't...fulfilled.

No surprise, she wasn't buying it. "What does that mean, satisfied?"

"It means exactly what I've said. I'm content. Life is good." He pulled out a chair, scraping the paved patio noisily. "Really good." Grabbing the water bottle he'd left out here, he tipped it back and doused a throat that had been dry since he'd opened the door and seen...her.

He hadn't been sure at first. She'd looked different. Natural. Plain, even, if that was possible. A tad older, but not a bit less perfect in his eyes. Even if she was a—

"I asked you a question, Ezekiel."

She had? "Sorry."

Exasperated, she dropped into a chair across the table. "What makes your life so good? That...that two-hundred-foot boat you have?"

"One hundred. And it's technically a yacht."

She rolled her eyes. "Oh, maybe it's one of the six houses you pay for in all those different countries."

"Four, and they're all paid off. And not that many countries, Mom. Two are in the U.S." And one in St. Barts and another in the south of France. Why *wasn't* he happy?

"Then is it all that autographed old baseball equipment you're always buying?"

He laughed at her description of one of the world's most expensive and extensive sports memorabilia collections. "Babe Ruth's 1920 Yankees jersey? Mark McGwire's seventieth home-run baseball? You know I love that stuff."

"Fifty million dollars' worth?"

"Sixty," he corrected. "I did a little shopping last month."

"And that's all you want out of life?"

No. He wanted laughter in his quiet houses and a family on his empty yacht and a partner in his massive bed. He wanted wholeness in a life that should have been overflowing but felt utterly...hollow.

"Ezekiel?" she urged.

He opened his mouth to answer, but of course no lie would come out. "I can't, Mom."

"You can." She leaned closer. Love and concern etched lines on her face as she lowered her voice. "You can try again."

He shook off the advice. "I mean I can't lie."

"Of course not. So these baseballs and boats and houses don't make you happy?"

He tipped the nearly empty water bottle in a fake toast, silent.

She nodded. "I thought as much. Your father is turning seventy, Ezekiel."

"I know, that's why I'm here, remember?" He pointed toward the list, happy for the change of subject. "Are you finished with the table...organizing?" He really had no idea what she was doing and couldn't care less, but he got to Florida so rarely, he owed her some attention.

She lifted a shoulder. "I thought of a few more last-minute additions. You know, some friends of mine—*and their daughters*—who I think I should add."

"Please don't do that, Mom. I do not want this party to turn into an army of eligible bachelorettes."

She waved a hand and leaned forward. "I hope it doesn't give your father a heart attack to walk into a restaurant and see a hundred people all there for him."

Zeke eyed her, trying to gauge if that was a particularly adept subject change or a hint at information he hadn't yet been able to get out of her. "Something wrong with his heart?" Last year, it had been the hip replacement. The year before, cataract surgery.

She trained her eyes on him. "Ezekiel, we're not exactly spring chickens, you know. We want to see the Nicholas name continue."

Guilt and grandchildren. Man, she was in her element now. "Aaaand we're back to the subject of the missing grandchildren." He let his head drop forward like he'd been clocked.

"Don't you smart-mouth me, young man. They are missing! Your brother had to marry that woman who refuses to give up one minute of her job at a bank so I could have a grandchild."

He chuckled at how she made Laura sound like a teller. "Mom, Jerry's wife is the CEO of one of the largest credit unions in the world. And they're happy without children."

"Are you?" she demanded.

"Happy without children or a CEO of a credit union?"

She glared at him. "Stop with the disrespectful mouth. I'm not one of your lackeys. You know what I mean. How long are you going to live this…" She flung a hand at the world in general. "Devil-may-care lifestyle of yours?"

Sometimes he was so lonely he wondered if even the devil did care about him. "Until I find the right person," he admitted. Maybe he'd choose better next time.

Mom sat back and crossed her arms, flattening him

with the same look he'd get when she'd find him awake in his room until three AM doing partial differential equations for fun. She knew what had happened; hell, she'd been there. Only, she didn't know the gory details. Still, she never stopped hoping that next time it could be different, even if she refused to even say the name of his—

"Well, you're going to be happy to know that I'm doing something about this situation."

He wasn't happy about anything in that sentence. Not the tone, not the fact that she was doing something, not even the reality that there was a *situation*. "What are you doing or shouldn't I ask?"

"I'm…" She let her voice drift off and looked down at the pages. "I've really got some terrific prospects picked out to come to the party."

"Mom, please. I really don't want you meddling—"

"Meddling! I'm your mother. I'm helping, not meddling."

She didn't know the difference between the two. "There's nothing to do, Mom. Honestly, I'm hap…" The lie stuck like dirt in his mouth. "I'm fine."

"Oh, you're fine all right." She stood suddenly, as if the chair couldn't contain her any longer. "You're so fine you are going to spend every day and night alone, and I am never going to rock a grandbaby." She loosened her arms to make a cradle. "You know, Ezra is a very popular name now."

This from a woman who'd named her sons Jeremiah and Ezekiel. "Mom." He stood slowly. "I date a lot."

"Dating isn't love!"

"No shit." He regretted the words the minute he'd mumbled them.

"Because you've dated the wrong women!" She came around the table, falling into the chair next to him so she could grab his arms and squeeze. "We're going to find you a nice girl. Not one of these skinny supermodels I see on those society pages with you. I'm going to find you a good, sweet, nurturing woman to be the mother of your children."

"Mom, honestly, I'm okay without turning Dad's party into *The Bachelor*."

"I don't think you're okay. Look at you."

Inching back, he gave her a shocked look. "What about me?"

"All you do is make money and go to that gym and keep getting…" She grabbed his bicep and tried to close her hand around it, which of course was impossible. "Is it necessary to be this muscular? Are you trying to kill people with these arms?"

He laughed and shook her off. "Just staying in shape."

"You know what keeps you in shape? Babies keep you in shape! A family keeps your heart in shape." She slapped a palm over her chest, smacking it loudly. "I know this is right, Ezekiel. That party will be like Cinderella's Ball, and you'll be the prince with his pick of the finest."

He didn't know whether to hoot or howl.

"Now, don't you give me that face, young man. I've been giving this a lot of thought. You'll have your choice of the loveliest girls on this island, in Naples, Fort Myers, oh, heck, I know people with eligible daughters in Miami Beach!"

He rearranged the look of shock and horror into a serious scowl. "Mom, I do *not* want to be hounded by a

24

bunch of gold-digging females who are trying to snag a husband. That's not why I'm here. I'm here for you, and Dad."

"And your business meetings."

"Yes, I have a few things scheduled with clients while I'm here, but honestly, I'm not here to…" He stood up, corralling his frustration. As he did, he caught the sound of something from the balcony above, outside one of the upstairs bedrooms.

The doors were open up there. How much had she heard?

"That's just the maid," his mother said.

He looked up and caught a flash of honey-colored hair inside the upstairs sliding glass door. Even in a maid's uniform, with no makeup, and clunky sneakers, she was sheer perfection. But, then, Mandy Mitchell could wear a burlap sack, and he'd want to get in it with her.

"Are you even looking, Ezekiel?"

"I am." And looking at her was still one of his favorite pastimes on Earth. He'd sat in the same classroom with Mandy Mitchell exactly twice in four years—not that she remembered—and the tilt of her nose, the angle of her jaw, and even the arches of her eyebrows over jade-green eyes were burned into his every synapse.

"You're not looking in the right places, then," his mother said pointedly.

"Yes, I am."

When his mother didn't answer, he caught her following his gaze, and then she sighed. "Such a sad story, that Mandy Mitchell."

"What's the story?" He tried to sound

disinterested, but hated how much he needed to know.

"You remember her from Mimosa High, right? The beauty queen, head cheerleader, prom princess, you know."

He knew. "Yeah."

She shook her head, tsking softly. "She got married right after college. Married quite well, too, they say."

He snorted. "Not well enough."

"Oh, he left her with *nothing*."

"She's divorced?" He had to work not to keep the elation out of his voice.

His mom tsked loudly but kept her voice at a whisper. "Dumped, more like. She probably cheated on him because what woman leaves a marriage with nothing?"

Plenty of women did—if a man did a prenup properly. His lawyer had mentioned it on more than one occasion.

But his mother was still relaying Mandy's story. "One day, she was a socialite in Tampa and the next, she was back in Mimosa Key, living in her parents' house on Sea Breeze Drive, while they gallivant all over the country in an RV."

Mandy wasn't married. The words ricocheted through his head.

"And have you seen her up close?" his mother asked. "Maybe it's me, but she sure doesn't look like the stunner she once was. It's like she stopped caring."

Maybe her skin didn't glow like polished porcelain and her eyes didn't have an artist's palette painted on them, and maybe she wasn't wearing a miniskirt that made his teenage boy's body take over every thought. But none of that was what made Mandy Mitchell beautiful to him.

His mother's attention was back on the lists. "You're going to like Elizabeth MacMann. Her father is a dentist, you know, in Naples. They belong to our club."

The country club in Naples. The dentists. The daughters. It all sounded like hell right now. Overhead, he heard the vacuum start up.

His mother stood. "Let's go have lunch so that girl can do the downstairs."

"I'm not that hungry, Mom." Not as long as he'd have a chance to talk to Mandy.

She eyed him harshly. "Why are you lying?"

"I'm not lying," he denied hotly.

"Well, something has you looking...hungry. Yes, I know that look in your eyes, son. You need some nourishment. I want to go before your father calls me to pick him up at his physical therapy. Let's go."

"All right." Reluctantly, he got up, realizing he was hungry. But not for food.

The question was, how was he going to satisfy that hunger?

Chapter Three

When she heard the front door close, Amanda hustled to the window to see Zeke let his mother in the passenger side of the car, then go round to get behind the wheel and drive away.

Only then did she let out the breath she'd been holding all the while she'd cleaned…and listened.

Hey, the sliders were open right over the patio. The conversation had drifted up. And…

He had a *fifty-million-dollar sports memorabilia collection*? A yacht? Four homes? And…he wasn't happy?

No, he hadn't said that, not once. But anyone with a brain, heart, and an ounce of knowledge about human nature could hear that between the lines. Well, shoot, what did it take to make someone happy, then?

She knew what his mother's answer would be. It was all Amanda could do not to break into a chorus of "Matchmaker, Matchmaker" after listening to that.

Well, at least he hadn't married one of his supermodel actress tabloid ladies and tried to bend, fold, and mutilate her into a woman he thought was perfect. Not like some powerful men she knew.

But a guy who looked like that and had cash out the wazoo? "Spare me," she whispered to herself as she lugged her bucket and mop downstairs. "Trouble with a capital T. So he's rich, big deal. Money doesn't buy you happiness."

It could, however, buy the business that would save her from having to work for Tori.

The thought meandered around her head as she walked down the hall to the master bedroom. Shame she'd been too shortsighted and status-conscious to have become friends with Ezekiel the Geekiel. Now she could have asked him for a loan.

She paused and got down on her knees, spying some dust along the baseboard. A guy with four houses and millions in "old sports equipment"—he wouldn't miss five grand. Pushing up, she headed into the master, where the plantation shutters remained closed, keeping the oversized room dim and cool.

The bed was unmade, a single leather duffle bag open at the bottom to reveal neat piles of clothes still packed inside. As she stripped the bed, the soft, masculine scent of him drifted up. Unable to resist, she pressed the empty pillowcase to her nose and sniffed, closing her eyes and remembering how he'd looked when he'd admitted his real name.

Shy. Humble. Hot as freaking hell.

She tossed the case onto the pile of sheets and went to the linen closet for a fresh set. Too bad she wasn't a woman without morals. She could…do him for five grand. The thought made her laugh out loud, but, damn, after it got planted, she couldn't help thinking about it.

She smoothed the fitted sheet, pulling the fine Egyptian cotton taut over the mattress. She took a second to let her finger caress the creamy linen, closing her eyes to imagine that man in this bed, naked, ready, hard... A completely unexpected and lusty thrill wended through her, giving a sharp jolt of desire she hadn't felt in a very, very long time.

Nice to know her bastard husband hadn't wrung *everything* out of her.

Finishing the bed, she turned to the bathroom, which should surely cool her inappropriate thoughts. Passing a two-person marble Jacuzzi, she stepped into the massive shower, looking along the wall at the six jets on either side—to accommodate two people, of course—all the way eight or ten feet high where, oh, damn it. Really?

A tiny little dragonfly clung to the tile, fluttering translucent wings. She let out a soft grunt. How did that get up there?

It didn't matter. Amanda had to get him down. Aiming carefully, she tried tossing her sponge at him and nearly grazed his wing, but he flew around the top of the shower and perched on the rain-shower nozzle in the ceiling.

"Oh, you're going to be sorry you didn't cooperate, buddy," she whispered to him. "This shower ain't big enough for the two of us."

She didn't have her step stool, so Amanda glanced around and spied the bucket she'd brought in. "That'll work." Turning it over, she checked the stability, which was good enough for a quick swipe, and placed a sneaker on it to hoist herself higher. "Hey, little guy." She waved at the dragonfly, hoping that would get him to fly down. "Come here. Come down to Mama."

On her tiptoes, she reached, but the dragonfly leaped from the wall and buzzed her. Amanda let out a soft cry and nearly toppled, grabbing hold of the wall to prevent a fall.

And DragonBastard flew back to the very top of the shower, ten feet in the air, his buzzy wings laughing at her.

"And now you die," she said, unhooking the faucet hose that was meant to make showering easy and luxurious but was about to drown an insect. Climbing up on the bucket again, she took aim with one hand, twisted the water on with the other, making the spray shoot forward with so much force it shook her whole body, wobbled the bucket, and all hope of balance.

Like it was happening in slow motion, Amanda felt herself suspended in midair for a split second, then down she went, slamming onto marble and losing hold of the spray hose that danced and twirled and soaked her from head to toe.

Slipping on the wet marble, she reached up to twist off the faucet, accidentally hitting the other knob, and instantly all twelve jets spewed ice-cold water.

"Holy, holy crap!"

"You need some help?"

She squeezed her eyes shut against the water and the horrible possibility that she'd heard a real voice, a human voice, a man's voice. Unless that flipping dragonfly could talk.

The water stopped. Shit. No dragonfly could do that.

"I call this above and beyond the call of cleaning duty."

She let out a soft sigh and finally opened her eyes, looking up at the silhouette of a man looming over her. Even blinded by water in her eyes, Amanda recognized the width of his shoulders and the soft lock of black hair

32

that fell near a blue eye. And, of course, a sly smile he couldn't fight.

As she opened her mouth to reply, the dragonfly buzzed down, right in front of Zeke's face. He snagged the insect with one quick snap of his wrist, careful not to crush him.

"Normally, I'd take this outside to live another day, but from the sound of things, you have a personal beef with him. Want me to squeeze the life out of him?"

Like the sight of this man was squeezing the life out of her lungs? Nothing—not even the DragonBastard—should suffer like that. She shook her head. "He may live."

"How about you?" With his other hand, he reached down.

"I may die of embarrassment." She pushed up on one knee, but he closed his hand over her elbow to help her up.

"Don't die until you dry off." His gaze dropped over her uniform, slowly enough that she couldn't help imagining the soaking wet cotton clinging like a second skin to her body. He lingered for a second on her breasts, definitely not reading her name tag this time. Under his gaze, she felt her nipples bud like little traitors.

"I call it a sign you throw yourself into your work. Literally."

Despite the chill of cold water trickling over every inch, heat rose to her cheeks. "I try," she said, attempting a smile.

He returned it as he helped her stand, backing up with the dragonfly fluttering madly in his other hand. "Let me take him out."

When he disappeared, Amanda nearly folded right

back down on the wet marble. What was she going to do now? She glanced down at the thin, wet, nearly see-through fabric and swore softly. Wouldn't that be a nice sight for resort guests as she walked back down the path! No doubt, that would get back to her boss.

She stepped out of the shower stall, unable to avoid a glance in the mirror. Her heart dropped like she just had from the upside-down bucket.

Tori's words echoed. *Have you looked at yourself lately?*

Sopping hair, soaked face, drenched uniform, and…oh, nothing about the woman gazing back from the mirror was *magnificent*.

Hearing his footsteps, she stepped away from the depressing sight and inhaled, digging deep for cool and composure.

"Would you like something dry to wear?" he asked, filling the bathroom doorway.

The question threw her, so unexpected and kind. Any other guest would have been furious at the intrusion and insisted she leave, right after they reported her to management.

"I'm…" She ran her hands over her torso. "I'll be out of here in a minute and send a…better maid."

"That's crazy. There's a clothes dryer here, right?"

Her pulse kicked, and not just because the offer was so damn thoughtful and the man delivering it was as handsome as he was sincere. It was so…unexpected. "In the laundry room, but I—"

"Then we'll have those dry in ten minutes." He reached for the knob to close the door. "There's a robe in the closet, but I'm sure you know that."

Without another word, he closed the door and left her

34

standing in stunned shock. Really? No chastisement for her incredible clumsiness and stupidity? No derisive look that he didn't get better service for all this money?

Grateful to the point of shaking, she slowly undressed, trying not to think about the fact that she could—no, she would—get fired if she got caught undressing in a guest's bathroom.

She slipped off her ID lanyard and set it on the counter, then unbuttoned the shirt, peeling the wet fabric from her body. Kicking off her sneakers, she did the same to the slacks, opting to keep her underwear but tossing in her water-logged bra.

She stepped into the robe and pulled out her ponytail, toweling her hair in the mirror, where things weren't that much better than they'd been a minute ago. Touching her pale cheeks, she leaned closer, seeing her face through his eyes.

Mandy the Mess.

She pinched her cheeks to return some color and licked her finger, blinking in an attempt to darken her pale lashes. But that didn't work. Then she remembered that inches from her hand, in the top drawer, was the complimentary makeup kit that management supplied in every bathroom in Casa Blanca. One of the perks of a resort owned by a woman, she'd often thought.

Very slowly, she tugged at the handle and pulled out the drawer, seeing the makeup, sunscreen, and some personal items.

It had been a long time since Amanda had bothered to put on makeup for a man. So why start now? She closed the drawer harder than necessary. What was she doing, anyway? Trying to impress a rich man? Hadn't she learned her lesson about men like that the hard way?

Scooping up her wet clothes, she opened the door, wearing a bathrobe and no mask.

Amanda found Zeke in the laundry room, the dryer wide open and waiting. He was staring straight ahead, his thoughts so far off and intense that he didn't hear her behind him. She paused for a second, taking him in, from the soft black hairs that brushed his collar to the strong, muscular back that pulled an expensive white shirt tight across his shoulders. His waist was narrow, the shirt tucked into crisp khaki pants, and his ass…

She let out a sigh. That right there ought to be illegal.

He spun around and caught her, sending a rush of shame to her cheeks. "Sorry, I…" Flustered, she walked to the dryer. "I can do this."

"No, please, give them to me." He reached for the ball of wet uniform, his hands closing over hers. She caught his gaze, locked on her, and they stood for the span of two, three, four strong heartbeats.

"I can do it, Zeke," she said quietly. Almost reluctantly, he lifted his hands from hers but didn't look away. "My guess is you don't run a lot of the dryers in your house…houses. Four, is it?"

His gaze flickered away. "You were listening."

"No, no. I did catch a little of your conversation, though." She shouldered him to the side and leaned over to toss her clothes in the dryer. "Your mom is…"

"Relentless," he supplied with a laugh, crossing his arms as he leaned on the granite folding counter next to the dryer. "It's a family trait."

"Is that how you account for your success?" she asked, bending over to unhook a button that had gotten caught inside the dryer.

"Might be, yeah. I get what I go after."

The smokiness in his voice made her turn in time to see his gaze on the gap in her robe. Slowly, she stood, tightening the robe, her stomach plummeting like she was on a roller coaster.

"And apparently you have a fondness for...sports equipment." She attempted a lightness despite the blood singing in her head.

"I have my weaknesses."

"Like most rich men," she muttered, turning away.

"Excuse me?"

She froze in midstep on her way out of the tiny laundry room, already feeling breathless from the lack of space and the growing heat from the dryer. "Never mind, I'm...I guess I'll..."

"What? Clean in your bathrobe?" He stayed leaning against the counter, his arms still crossed, amusement tugging at the corners of his eyes. "What did that comment mean, exactly?"

"It was me being a little bitchy," she admitted. "Which is totally out of line considering how easily you could get me fired for this."

His face softened. "I would never do that."

"Thank you. And, anyway, I seem to be well on my way to doing that all by myself."

"Because you had a little run-in with the shower hose? You don't give yourself enough credit, Mandy."

She smiled at the sound of her name on his lips, so sweet it actually made her next breath come out shakily.

Or maybe that was the size and closeness of him and the way his whole face shifted from handsome to heartbreaking when he smiled.

"I give myself plenty of credit," she said. "In fact," she added with a dry laugh, "I'm basically living on the stuff now."

He lifted an eyebrow in interest.

"Not that someone like you could appreciate that, but..." Why had she told him this? Because she wanted pity? Help? A loan? A little disgusted with herself, she started to turn, but he reached out and snagged her elbow.

"Don't leave."

"I...can't really, well, go anywhere," she said. "But maybe I could dust."

He laughed, still holding her elbow and inching her closer. "There's no dust. Tell me about how you are getting yourself fired."

"You really want to know?"

"Yes." He let go and propped his hands on the counter at his back, the knuckles nearly white, she noticed, as if he were forcing himself to hang on and not touch her.

Oh, Amanda Lockhart, what an imagination you have.

"Well, it looks like we're having a management change, and I'm not going to make the first staffing cut when we do."

His features shifted to a concerned frown. "Really? Are you sure?"

"Positive."

"I'll give you a good recommendation. Will that help?"

She let out a breath of surprise and gratitude at the offer. "That's so sweet. I'd love to read that letter, too. 'Amanda's strengths include pest control, eavesdropping, and water management.'"

He laughed. "But she looks damn fine in my bathrobe."

She opened her mouth to reply, but whatever she was going to say got stuck in her throat. Because…that wasn't true. "I thought I heard you tell your mother you don't lie."

"I don't." His eyes grew darker blue, all mirth disappearing as his expression shifted to dead serious. "I really never lie. I deal in numbers and facts for a living, and numbers and facts never lie."

She waited for him to continue, lost in the way he spoke with authority and the shape of his mouth every time it moved. His lips were…perfect. Under the soft velveteen of the robe, she burned with a slow, tingling heat that was definitely not caused by the dryer.

"Well, you're lying now," she said, her voice surprisingly gruff. "Because I don't look fine. I look wet and…tired. And…" *Broken*. "I've had some tough years."

"They don't show," he said, as factually as if he'd added two plus two. "In fact, I can't take my eyes off you."

For a long moment, she didn't say anything, but tried to swallow, her throat tight and dry. Was he being honest, this man who claimed to never lie? It sure seemed that way, but—

"And there was a time," he said, slowly taking his hands off the counter as though he trusted himself to be steady now, "when I couldn't look right at you."

She blinked at him.

"It was like looking at the sun," he whispered, taking one step closer. "So bright and so blinding that it hurt." In front of her, he gently put his hands on her shoulders, holding her perfectly still in the doorway. "And you know how when you look at the sun, you can't see straight for an hour? You have spots in your eyes and everything else in the world is gray?"

It sounded honest. It sounded…lovely. Somehow, she managed to nod, any hope of a reply trapped in her hammering chest.

"Looking right at you used to do that to me." His thumbs grazed her collarbone, the touch so light she almost had to close her eyes and let the electrical impulses rock her. "It still does."

"Now I know you're…" *Lying*. He had to be lying. Saying whatever he thought he had to say to get this robe off. "Different."

"From high school?" He lifted a brow. "Yeah. I'm different. Back then I couldn't talk to you without wanting to fold in half. Now I can't talk to you without…" He lowered his head, inches from her face. "Mandy."

She closed her eyes then, the sound of her name on those beautiful lips like music and rainfall and thunder and…

Softness. His kiss was so soft, it shocked her. His grip grew tighter, his lips hungrier, and a low, masculine catch in his throat was as seductive as a stroke of his fingertips.

He flicked his tongue, she angled her head. He eased her closer, she bowed her back. He pressed against her, and she—

Shoved him away with a grunt. "Don't!" Fury and fear clutched at her, twisting with way more force than desire had. What the hell was *wrong* with her?

He blinked, jerking his hands in the air like a caught criminal. "I'm...shit, Mandy, I'm..." He swallowed, shaking his head. "I'm not sorry, but I really didn't mean to..."

"To what? Kiss me? Undress me? Sweet-talk me with some...some bullshit about the sun?"

His eyes darkened. "I told you I don't lie."

"Well, I don't generally make out with the guests." *Except the ones who make me lose my mind.* "I feel like some kind of...I don't know." But she did know. There was a word for women who did what she'd been thinking about since she'd laid eyes on him. An ugly word.

"God, I'm so sorry." And he looked it, too. His brows drawn together, his eyes raw with self-disgust, his hands dropping to his sides.

"That's what you guys do," she said, old but certainly not dead emotions bubbling up inside. "You make a woman think she's special and then you want to...destroy her."

His eyes widened. "Mandy—"

She held up both hands. "Nobody calls me that anymore." She pivoted and marched out, not sure where she was going, but she couldn't take that tiny space and giant man anymore. Everything vibrated—her head, her body, her heart, her memories.

He wasn't like Doug—or was he?

She crossed the living room, heading to the other side of the house. She'd hide in the bedroom until her clothes were—

"Amanda." He snagged the robe sleeve. "Please, let me

41

talk to—"

She jerked her arm so hard she slipped right out of the sleeve, but he held on and the robe fell open, revealing her nakedness and pulling a soft shriek from her mouth.

The click of the front door reverberated, like a bullet shot underwater. In slow, shocked motion, they both turned, speechless as the door flew open and hit the wall.

"Housekeep—" Tori froze in the doorway, her eyes wide. "Well, would you look at that?"

Before Amanda could scramble back into the robe, a bald head appeared behind Tori and JT's eyes damn near sprang out of his head, too. "Whoa, Amanda. That's probably a little more customer service than we generally offer."

Chapter Four

I n one lightning-fast move, Zeke slipped Mandy back into her robe, getting close enough to feel her whole body trembling. What an idiot he was! He couldn't keep his hands off her for five minutes? Now she was as white as that robe.

"Who the hell are you?" he demanded of the morons who'd just barged in. "Can't a guest expect privacy?"

The woman sauntered in, appraising him up and down like some kind of hungry hooker. "We're with housekeeping doing a room check. You're supposed to be at lunch."

"Guess Amanda's dessert." The meathead behind her loped in and grinned. "Sorry for the inter—"

Zeke took two steps and had the guy's collar before he could take his next breath. "What did you say?"

"Hey, hey, sorry, sir." He held up his hands and shook his head, fear in his eyes. He should have been afraid for that comment. "We were told to check on this villa because Amanda isn't exactly the best house—"

Zeke tightened his grip and lifted the guy a half inch off the ground.

"Zeke, please." Mandy's voice cracked with the plea.

Slowly, he let the guy drop but continued to slice him with a look that he knew communicated exactly how much pleasure he'd get from throwing him against the wall. "You can leave now."

The other woman put her hands on her hips and shook her head at Mandy. "Honey, you know we gotta tell Lacey about this."

"It's not what it looks like," Mandy said.

The woman gave a sharp laugh. "Well, it sure doesn't look like cleaning to me."

Zeke whipped around and glared at her, but she looked up and smiled. "Not that I can blame the girl."

"Hey," the other man said harshly. "Let's go, T."

"And leave her here?" She tsked. "I am certain there are legal ramifications and employee guidelines and every other manner of professional misbehavior being displayed. Amanda, dear, why don't you find your clothes from wherever you dropped them, and we'll ride you back to the management office?"

Zeke was in her face in one second. "Why don't you shut your mouth and get your skinny ass out of this villa before I call the cops?"

She flinched a little, then shot a look at Mandy. "Got yourself a hothead, darlin'. I heard you like them with a little fire in the belly."

Zeke inhaled so hard he felt his nostrils quiver, and the woman had the good sense to slink away.

"We'll see you in Lacey's office," she said, backing out of the door just before Zeke slammed it in her face and flipped the deadbolt and guest lock. Only then did he turn to survey the damage.

But Mandy was gone.

He shot through the kitchen and stopped cold at the

laundry room door at the sight of her back to him, naked but for pink underpants, as she tried to hook her bra.

"Go away," she said.

He stepped into the kitchen to give her privacy. "I feel like shit," he said.

"You got Tori to leave."

Tori? "Tori Drake?" He knew she looked vaguely familiar.

"The one and only. And she's made a career out of getting back at me for being on the homecoming court when she was the one servicing the football players."

Damn, it was like a high school reunion around here. "I shouldn't have...I shouldn't have touched you."

She didn't answer, and he banged his head against the wall behind him, squeezing his eyes shut. *Son of a bitch!* "I don't suppose I could make this up to you."

"Five thousand would do the trick."

His eyes popped open. "*What*?"

"Never mind, I'm making a joke in a very unfunny situation." He heard a zipper slide and the rustle of more clothes. "I told you I was on the way out of this job anyway."

He stepped into the doorway as she buttoned the top button. "That may or may not be true, but I'll be damned if you are going to lose your job because I acted like an asshole."

"You weren't an asshole," she said softly. "You're just a man."

Which was obviously one and the same to her. Damn it, he was such a moron. "Mandy."

She looked up from the button, adding a punch to his gut when he saw the dampness of her eyes. "Sorry, I'm a little bitter. I left my sneakers in the bathroom. Excuse me." She brushed by him and left him standing like a helpless, hopeless idiot.

He heard her in the living room and pushed off the wall, refusing to let her leave without saying goodbye. She was sitting on the sofa, tying her shoes, her blonde hair, dry now, hanging like corn silk in front of her face.

He took a slow step closer. "I told you I am honest, probably to a fault."

She didn't look up.

"So you should know that what I'm about to say is true and not some asshole guy spouting bullshit because he wants to get laid."

She knotted the lace, silent.

"I had a crush on you in high school that pretty much crippled me at the sound of your name."

Her hands stilled.

"I couldn't..." He gave a dry laugh. "I couldn't breathe when you were in the room."

Very slowly, she lifted her face to him.

"I know you were...like royalty. And I was not. And I know now, as a man, that none of that matters. But I want to tell you this."

She stared at him, waiting as he walked up to her and got down on one knee so they were face to face.

"Once, when we were freshmen, some kid mowed me down in the hall and knocked all my books and my sixteen different calculators and protractors to the floor. You stopped and got down, like this, and helped me pick up every single thing. And when that kid laughed at you, do you know what you said?"

Her green eyes still swam in tears as she shook her head.

"You stood up and flattened him with a look and

said, 'Get to class because you obviously have none.'"

She started to smile. "I could be a real—"

He held up a hand, silencing her. "Angel. I thought you were an angel. I thought you were..." He swallowed. "Obviously too good for me."

"Zeke, I..."

He looked down and took the laces of the other shoe, slowly tying them for her. When he'd knotted them, he looked into her eyes again. "You told me a few minutes ago that I was relentless."

She nodded.

"Wait until you see the power of that."

He heard her suck in a quiet breath. That was good. He wanted to take her breath away. And he would. She just didn't know that yet.

The sun spilled into the Gulf that evening, turning the water a thousand shades of gold and pink, tinged with violet, topped with twilight. As Zeke walked barefoot over the sand of Barefoot Bay, he barely noticed nature's artwork. His head down, he turned the hard piece of plastic hanging on a yellow lanyard over in his hand and read the name for the hundredth time.

Amanda Lockhart.

She'd left her ID and master key in his bathroom, which would probably be yet another transgression against her. His trip to the management offices found them closed for the evening, but he wasn't about to give this key up to some lackey at the front desk. Whoever

"Lacey" was, he was going to find her, and finally, he'd bumped into a talkative, friendly, and quite attractive young woman who'd identified herself as the owner of the resort's hot-air-balloon business.

Zoe Bradbury had had an enchanting personality, and when she'd found out he was the guest staying in Bay Laurel, she'd made one call, and sent him up the beach to the owners' house. He appreciated people who could get things done and had told her so.

The Walkers, who evidently designed, built, owned, and managed the resort, lived in a two-story stucco home covered with ivy and facing the water at the very northernmost end of the bay. A stroller was parked next to a truck and a golf cart in the circular drive, and as he reached the property, the front door opened and a red-haired woman in a crisp white shirt and jeans stepped out to greet him.

"Mr. Nicholas?" Concern tinged her voice, and her brows pulled over amber eyes, confirming that most resort guests weren't typically given this kind of access to the owners. Good. He wasn't most resort guests.

"Mrs. Walker?" Holding the badge in his left hand, he reached out his right and they shook. "Please call me Zeke."

"I'm Lacey. I understand we had an incident in your villa today. Would you like to come in?"

He heard the playful squeal of a baby behind her and shook his head. "I don't need to invade your home, ma'am. I merely want to clear a few things up, and I can do that right here."

She crossed her arms and nodded, the breeze picking up a strawberry-colored curl from her shoulder. "Please do."

"Mand...Amanda left this." He handed her the ID and card key, and she closed her eyes, obviously not happy. "After she nearly killed herself trying to get a dragonfly out of the shower and accidentally turned on the water and got soaked through to the bone."

She looked up, a question in her eyes.

"I don't lie."

A smile flickered. "I believe you."

"I hope you do and not the two people who stormed my rented villa—without announcing themselves, I might add—and assumed the worst, which was completely wrong."

She swallowed, processing this. "You have to admit it was an extremely awkward situation."

"Awkward, but not what it appeared."

She nodded slowly. "I've talked to Amanda."

"And?"

"I had to let her go," she said unapologetically. "No matter how or why her uniform was wet, wearing a guest's robe and staying in the villa is unacceptable behavior for a housekeeper." Her eyes tapered, and he caught the accusation.

"I persuaded her to stay. We knew each other at Mimosa High."

"You went to Mimosa High?"

"Class of '02."

A warm smile, the first he'd seen, lit her face. "Well, I'm a few years older than you, but I'm a Scorpion, too." Then she frowned, shaking her head. "I didn't know Amanda was an alum, but then, I really have only talked to her at length one other time."

"Then you don't know that she's not at all like what those other employees assumed."

She toyed with the card key, sighing. "They're not only employees," she said. "They are actually the winners of a bid I put out a few months ago. I'm planning to outsource my housekeeping function to one company, and they've got the job. I need to trust them."

Realization dawned. "So that's why Amanda told me she'd be fired shortly."

Lacey's eyes flashed. "Why would she assume...really?" She tapped the plastic key against her hand, thinking. "I didn't know this situation was brewing," she admitted. "And it makes me all the sorrier I couldn't help Amanda when she came to me."

"Instead, you fired her."

"No, no. Not today. Awhile back. She wanted the outsourcing business," she said. "And she seems to have the brains and ambition, so I told her she'd be in the running if she could get a business off the ground. But, sadly, it does take working capital to start something like that, and she couldn't—"

"How much?"

She lifted her brows and gave a shrug. "I'm not sure, but the proposal she'd put together looked like she'd need a cash infusion of about five thousand dollars, so more than she has, I'm afraid."

Five thousand would do the trick.

Her words played on his memory. "Can't she get a small-business loan?" he asked.

"I'm sorry, Zeke, I really don't know her personal situation, but—"

"Don't you think you ought to know an employee's personal situation before you fire her?"

She drew back, her shoulders square. "She was found in a villa undressed with a guest. I'm running a first-class, five-star resort, and I make no apologies for my business decisions or employee relations."

In the entryway behind her, a man appeared, holding a baby who couldn't have been a year old. "Everything okay out here?"

"Yes," she said, indicating him. "This is Zeke Nicholas, our guest in Bay Laurel. Zeke, this is my husband, Clay Walker."

"The architect?" Zeke asked.

He nodded. "I designed the resort."

"I'm a fan of your work. I...I thought you were older."

Clay smiled, his blue eyes glinting with understanding. "My father's an architect, as well, and much better known than I am." He gave the baby a little pat. "And this is Elijah. We're hoping he picks up a drafting pencil soon, too."

Lacey laughed. "Not that soon."

Zeke gave the little guy a wink when he turned big blue eyes exactly like his daddy's on him. "Cute kid. And, look, about today? My side of the story is the truth."

"Thank you," Lacey said. "I appreciate you stopping by and returning the card key."

"I'm sorry to have interrupted your family time."

"I'm always available for guests," she said.

He started to leave, but stopped midstep. "Can I ask you one more question?"

The couple nodded in unison.

"Is your decision about the outsourcing of that business final?"

They shared a look, the kind that told him they talked about everything and didn't make any decisions in a vacuum.

"We've made a verbal agreement," Lacey said. "But nothing's signed. Why?"

"If Amanda were able to finance that business, would you give her a shot, in spite of what happened today?"

Lacey sighed, slowly shaking her head, but her eyes said she knew what he was suggesting. "Oh, I don't know. That would be—"

"Oh, Strawberry." Her husband shifted the baby to his other arm to get even closer to her. "How soon we forget."

"What?" she asked him.

He gave her a half smile and swiped a hand through near-shoulder-length, sun-streaked hair, an earring twinkling in his lobe. "I seem to recall a young woman who, not so long ago, had to do some pretty creative maneuvering to get her own business, and there were plenty of people who thought her track record didn't merit a second chance. Not to mention her relationship with one of her business partners."

Her face softened as she smiled at him, the connection between them palpable. After a second, she turned back to Zeke, her eyes shining. "Everyone deserves her shot, I suppose."

Zeke nodded. "That's all we'd ask."

A few minutes later, he was halfway down the beach on his way to his next stop before he realized he'd said "we."

Chapter Five

Amanda had a good shower cry. Ugly, hard, and stinging, even though she didn't get soap in her eyes.

When the water heater gave out, she finally dried off, slipped on a tank top and sleep pants and poured a glass—okay, a vat—of wine before heading into her room. Her *old* room, not the master she'd slept in for her year of free rent in exchange for house-sitting. Mom had long ago turned Amanda's teenage-girl room into a den/guest/catch-all combo, which had turned dusty and musty from lack of use. In every corner, the fading light left shadows…and memories.

This room might look different than it had when it was a teenager's sanctuary, but Amanda had left plenty of herself in here. Sleepovers, studying, and hours of…admiration. The closet doors were sliding full-length mirrors, trimmed in brass.

How many hours had Mandy Mitchell spent in front of her own reflection? God, she'd been self-absorbed. No wonder Tori hated her. Along with everyone else she'd probably treated like second-class citizens.

Except Ezekiel Nicholas. Had she really thrown that

"class" comment at a bully? She didn't remember having a caring bone in her body back then. But that's not how he saw her. And she didn't even remember the book-bag and bully incident.

Without taking even a glance at her reflection in the mirrored door, Amanda rolled it, searching the floor for the plastic container Mom had used to store what had been on the bookshelves.

Spotting the box, Amanda slid to the floor, taking a deep drink of wine before setting the glass on the nightstand. She had to find that yearbook.

As she dug through pieces of her life packed into a bin, she refused to let the nostalgia get to her. They were things from her bookshelves, that's all. Not *her*. A tiara from homecoming, a framed picture of her in her cheerleading uniform, a dried corsage from prom, the program from the Miss Teen Florida pageant—they were distant, ancient memories of a girl who no longer existed.

She should probably thank Doug for humbling her in their marriage, for years of put-downs and insults and reminders that he had the power and she was nothing but a wife. It hadn't taken long for Amanda's confidence to crumble. Now she was building it back up, but this time, she would leave the arrogance behind.

When she lifted the graduation cap, her fingers hit the hard edge of a book cover.

Mimosa High Yearbook 2002...A New Day Has Come

The edition was more serious than most years, less emphasis on partying at the beach and more emphasis on making a difference in the world. Of course, the first month of their senior year had been September of 2001, a time in history marred by events that had changed every heart in the world.

Amanda leaned back against the bed, reaching for another sip of wine before opening the book. Then she flipped to the seniors, and the pages automatically opened to the middle of the alphabet, with her picture on the left-hand side.

She ignored it and skimmed straight to the N's, stunned to see Ezekiel Nicholas directly underneath her.

"Holy crap," she whispered to herself. She didn't know what was more amazing—the fact that he'd gone from zero to a dime since they'd graduated or that she had never even noticed his picture under hers.

He was right under her on the same page, and she'd never even known he existed beyond a cutting nickname.

I thought you were an angel.

His confession still rang in her ears. After one of the most difficult, harrowing days of her life, when she'd actually been told: "I'm sorry, Amanda, but we have to let you go"—yet the only words that she wanted to think about from today were...*I thought you were an angel.*

She stared at his picture, able to see the early lines of what would become a handsome male jaw and those piercing blue eyes hidden by thick glasses. He wasn't smiling. Had anyone even talked to him? Had she ever again been nice to him?

The doorbell made her jump, pulling her from her reverie. That was Jocelyn Palmer, of course. Her neighbor who ran the Casa Blanca Spa hadn't been at the resort today when Amanda got fired, but no doubt she knew about everything, since she was very close friends with Lacey Walker.

She waited a minute, staring at Ezekiel the Geekiel a minute longer. She didn't really want to face her neighbor right now. She didn't want to admit she'd gotten herself in such a sticky situation with a resort guest that it had cost the job Jocelyn had helped her get.

The bell rang a second time, followed by a loud knock. On a sigh, Amanda pushed herself up, still holding the yearbook. She snagged the wine glass, as though that would prove just how bad she felt about losing her job.

At the end of the hall, she turned toward the living room, glancing out through the white sheers just as a figure walked away from the door.

A male figure. Frozen, Amanda stared at Zeke Nicholas. What was—

He turned at that instant and caught her looking before she could duck out of the way.

For a second, time froze as they stared at each other, then a slow, easy smile broke over his face that was as real and warm as the setting sun behind him. He pointed to the front door, and she let out the breath she'd been holding.

Oh, God. There was no reasonable way out of this, she supposed. She tucked the yearbook under her arm and opened the front door. He stayed on the walk, down two steps, so they were at eye level, but he was no less gorgeous and intimidating than when he had her by a good five or six inches.

For a moment, they stared at each other, and all she could think of was how much he'd changed since...

His eyes dropped, and she realized her tank top was just this side of see-through. She angled the yearbook over her chest. "I looked you up," she said, hoping that explained why she suddenly felt the need to shield herself with it.

"And I see I've driven you to drink."

She raised the glass. "Clearly, I'm having my own little pity party."

"No one should do that alone."

No one...should look that damn good after being positively invisible in high school. How had he done that?

She could practically feel his desire to move forward, like a horse held at the starting gate. "Can I come in?"

No. She could hear the word in her head, imagine how easy it would be to say, and how effective and right and smart and safe it would sound. Just...no. Simple. Two letters. One syllable.

"Of course you can." Or that.

He strode forward and up the steps, making her clutch the yearbook, determined to hold her ground and not back up. Except, now he was too close and too tall and too...much.

"You're under me," she said softly.

His eyes glinted with surprise. "Not at the moment."

"Right under me on the senior picture page. The L's, M's, and N's are on the same page and we...lined up."

"Really? I've never seen that yearbook." He reached for it. "May I?"

Well, he had seen her boobs for a flash already today. She relinquished the book and tried not to feel self-conscious about the thin material covering her. "You've never looked at our yearbook?"

"I didn't have great memories of high school."

She gestured toward the sofa. "Well, have yourself a stroll down memory lane then. Would you like a glass of wine?"

She watched him walk past her to sit down, placing the book on the table without opening it. "I'm all right, thanks."

That was an understatement. He still wore the same crisp khakis and five-hundred-dollar shirt he'd had on today, and he still looked perfect. He still smelled like summer in the woods. He still oozed power and control and testosterone, all those things she was determined to avoid.

She folded into a chair across the coffee table, crossing her arms and curling her legs under her, not asking the obvious question of why he was here but wanting to see how he'd open this conversation.

Sitting down, he leaned his elbows on his knees, steepling his long fingers right under his chin. "I understand you lost your job."

"Good news travels fast on Mimosa Key, as always."

He didn't say anything, looking directly at her. But why *was* he here? To apologize? To finish what he'd started? A slow heat traveled up her body. She damn well better get acquainted with the word "no" or she could qualify as the world's stupidest woman.

"You and I both know that's not good news. I feel really bad about what happened."

Yes, he was there to apologize. She could let her poor hormones rest now. "Thanks, but, honestly, it was inevitable. You—that, um, situation—forced me to move faster to find another job."

"What are you going to do?"

She lifted a shoulder. "I heard the Toasted Pelican is hiring waitresses. All the peanuts you can eat and rotgut you can drink."

He didn't smile at the local humor. "You need to start your own business."

She let out a soft laugh. "Yeah. That'd be nice." So would robbing a bank.

"I mean it."

"I know it," she replied, unnerved by more than his intense gaze. She couldn't breathe. How did he know this, anyway?

"I have a check for five thousand dollars in my pocket."

She stared at him, the words nearly doubling her over with their impact. "*What?*"

"I have a check for—"

"I heard you." She shot to her feet, indignation and fury and shock rocking through her body. "How? Why? What…why?"

He stood, too, instantly gaining the advantage of height. "Because you need it to start your business, and I'm the reason you don't have a job."

Her jaw hung open as she tried to piece together the puzzle and came up with…nothing that looked like a picture.

"I spoke to Lacey Walker," he said, obviously reading her confusion.

"*What?*"

"I spoke to—"

She swiped her hand through the air to silence him. "I heard you," she repeated through gritted teeth. "I don't believe what I heard, but…why would you do that?"

"You left your employee badge and master key in my bathroom."

The sting of embarrassment mixed with fury, tingling

her skin and sparking her nerves. "So you took it to the owner of the resort?"

He nodded, crossing his arms. "At her house. I met her husband, too, and their baby."

He'd gone to Lacey's house? "I'm dreaming, right?" She choked the words. "Tell me this is a nightmare. Any minute I'm going to wake up and realize this isn't happening, that I had a horrible day that has spilled into a really…bad…"

Her words faded as he reached out and brushed his knuckles along her jaw, sending a thousand goose bumps to join the chills of fury she already had. "Not a dream. I know what you want, and I have a check in my—"

"I don't want your damn money!" Jerking back from his touch, she practically spit the words at him.

"Mandy, I want to help you."

"In exchange for what?" She slammed her hands on her hips. "You want to buy sex? I'm sure there's plenty of places you can do that on the Internet or over on the mainland."

"Sex?" She had to give him credit, he looked pretty horrified. "I'm not here to buy sex."

"I admit," she said, anger still rolling through her veins like lightning. "You don't look like you need to do that, but, whoa, buddy. I know…people…guys…men like you have—"

"You don't know men like me." Now *he* sounded mad. Oh, that was rich.

"I do—"

"You think you know men like me. But I guarantee you, Mandy, you have never met anyone like me."

She opened her mouth to argue, then shut it, only

because of the raw sincerity in his voice and eyes. Maybe she *didn't* know a guy like him.

"I am not here to buy anything." He tunneled his fingers into his hair and slowly swiped it back, leaving it a little tussled and messy. And sexy as hell.

She closed her eyes, trying to look disgusted but really forcing her brain to cooperate and stop thinking of him that way. She *couldn't.*

"I feel incredibly responsible for your losing your job and...I told you this afternoon, you did me a favor a long time ago and I never forgot it. I know you need this money to get started and, hell, Mandy, I'll never miss it."

Lucky bastard. With a little grunt, she turned and headed into the kitchen to get away from the overwhelming sight of him. But of course he followed her. She stood at the sink, her fingers splayed on the porcelain, staring out at her mother's tiny backyard.

"I don't mean to sound so cavalier about money."

Judging from his voice he was about a foot behind her. Maybe two. Too close. She gripped the sink until her arms shook.

"But I give to charity and—"

She turned slowly, a rueful smile on her lips. "Charity? I guess that's not quite as bad as what I thought."

"Mandy." His eyes softened, and he lifted his hands in supplication. "I'm trying to help you."

And just like that, she felt everything melting. Her heart. Her fury. Her complete inability to trust anything with a Y chromosome. "I know," she whispered, hating that her voice cracked and her eyes stung. "I have...issues."

He managed a smile. "I noticed."

"I had a bad…marriage."

"I figured."

"He hurt me."

His eyes flashed. "I'm sorry."

"I kind of hate men."

He fought a smile. "I'm getting that."

"Especially men with money and power and…all that entails."

"I don't know what that entails, Mandy. I'm just a guy who's done really well in business, and that's turned into a lot of money."

"A *lot*," she repeated.

"A whole hell of a lot," he agreed. "I'm not going to apologize for that or for every asshole who doesn't know how to treat a woman." He reached into his pocket and pulled out a piece of paper—his check, no doubt. She didn't have the nerve to look at it or the wherewithal to take her eyes off his. "I have absolutely zero expectations from this and, if it will make you happy, we can consider it a loan with no interest and no due date."

"Which makes it a gift, not a loan."

His lips curved. "Semantics. Is that a yes?"

"No." She inched back, hitting the sink, her gaze slipping to his hand before returning to his face.

Five thousand dollars… from a drop-dead god of a man who could wield that power…

"You're thinking about it," he said, fluttering the check.

On a sigh, she looked again. "I could get bonded and buy equipment and rent the office and hire…oh." Disappointment thudded again. "Never mind. This is a waste of time."

62

"Why?" He stepped closer. "I can help you do all that stuff. I've started dozens of businesses."

The offer slayed her, it was so genuine. "I mean it's a waste of time because I need customers. Lacey will never give me the outsourcing business now, even if I could put the whole package together. She was so mad this afternoon, she was spitting nails. I'm done at Casa Blanca."

"I don't know about that," he said. "Her husband seemed reasonable, and she believed me when I told her what happened."

She searched his face, daring to hope, daring to dream. "Really? What did they say?"

"I wasn't quite sure, but I get the impression she's been in your shoes before, having to take a risk." He paused and gave her a meaningful look. "I get the impression her husband helped her."

"Oh, yeah. I've heard stories about how they met on the beach and fell in…" Her voice grew tight. They fell in love, got married, had a baby, and lived happily ever after.

Fairy tales that sure didn't happen to every woman.

"Anyway." Amanda waved off the thought. "I have to think about this."

"Bad idea." She could have sworn he took a step closer but didn't actually seem to move. Somehow, he was…trapping her. And, damn it, she liked it.

"Why?" she asked. "I have to think about it. I have to sleep on you, I mean, on it."

He grinned and pointed to her with the check. "You've got sex on the brain."

She had to laugh. "No, it was a slip of the tongue."

"Don't think about it, Mandy. You'll think yourself

right out of the offer. Take the money." He took her hand and tried to pry her palm open. "Make a business plan and—"

She kept her fingers squeezed. "I have a business plan."

"Good girl. Then put together a list of every step you have to—"

"I have that list." She was ready. The only thing stopping her was...pride and self-respect and... Her fingers slackened a bit. "It could take me years to pay you back."

"I don't care."

"I do." She let out another sigh, almost opening her hand, but this was...so wrong. "I'm going to feel like I owe you."

"You owe me nothing. I'm here for a week or so. I have some meetings and my dad's party and, other than that, I'll help—"

She snapped her fingers and pointed at him so hard and fast, he drew back an inch. "That's it!"

"What?"

She snapped again, over and over, unable to contain her happiness. "I know what I can do for your five thousand dollars."

"I don't need anything, Mandy."

"Oh, yes, you do." She tapped his chest playfully, already loving this idea. "You need a bodyguard."

"What?" He shook his head. "I'm not in any danger here. I've used bodyguards in certain countries, of course, but I don't need protection on Mimosa Key."

"Wanna bet?" She clapped her hands together, so completely happy with the idea. "You need someone to hold back the legions of single women your mother is prancing past you at that party."

His eyes lit and his jaw unhinged—the look of surprise and delight making him even more handsome, if that was possible. "You're right. I need a girlfriend for that event."

"Or at least a date."

"No, no, it would have to be official to get my mother off my case. But…"

"But she knows me and knows I'm a maid here, and she'd figure out in a New York minute that you're lying," she supplied, reading his expression.

"Except that I don't lie. Ever." He shook his head, his smile tight. "And she knows it. Because she has liedar."

Amanda choked. "Liedar?"

"The ability to smell a lie a mile away." He gave a self-deprecating laugh. "Of course, I am the world's crappiest liar."

"Oh, well. That's a shame because I really… liked the idea."

He was searching her face, thinking. "I love the idea."

The way he said it made her toes ball up on the tile floor. "Then you have to lie."

"Not if…it's true."

More toe-curling. "I'm not your girlfriend, Zeke."

"But what if we make it official? You are my girlfriend, and I am not lying."

Oh, that would be…not good. "Semantics," she echoed. "We obviously just met…" At his look, she conceded with a nod. "Okay, we knew each other in high school, but it's a stretch to say I'm your girlfriend and it not be at least a white lie. Can you tell one? Or can't I just be a really clingy date?"

His eyes narrowed, and he took one step closer. "No. There's a much simpler answer." Tipping her chin with one gentle finger, he lifted her face to his.

"Which is?"

He annihilated her with the intensity of his gaze, crazy-sky blue looking right through to her soul. "Mandy Mitchell, will you be my girlfriend?"

"Zeke...I..."

"Don't say no."

No, no, *no*. But not a word came out as he lowered his face and covered her mouth with the sweetest, softest, sexiest kiss she could ever remember.

Chapter Six

Zeke angled his head but purposely kept the kiss air-light, no more than a brush of a promise, because Mandy was about as secure in his touch as a wisp of smoke. Everything in him wanted to push her against that counter, crush her open-mouthed, and move his hands up and down the delicious body that was all too visible under the flimsy top.

But then she'd disappear. He knew that. But he lingered one second longer, taking one tingly taste of her lower lip. Only then did he back away. Her eyes were still closed, her lips parted, her chest rising and falling with one strangled breath. She'd flattened her hands on his chest, either ready to push or pull. He didn't know which.

"Now I won't be lying," he said softly. "You're my girlfriend."

She opened her eyes, the green rimmed with a darker emerald, her golden lashes fluttering up to her brows. "You'll...still be lying."

"Nope." He shook his head. "It's official. Sealed with a kiss."

"That's not enough."

He couldn't help smiling. "Oh, well, there's more where that came from."

"No, no…I…" She lifted her hands as if she suddenly realized she'd splayed them across his pecs. "I can't. It would be…wrong."

"Wrong? Why?"

"Because…I'm not…" She closed her eyes for a second, gathering her wits, slowly taking her hands to her sides, being careful not to touch him, as though he might burn her. "This has to be strictly business," she finally said. "Absolutely, unequivocally, no doubt about it…a business deal."

Which was about as sexy as a rock, but okay. Maybe he could get her to change her mind. Or maybe not.

"Strictly," she repeated, pointing a finger at him.

He tried to ignore the punch in his gut, but it was hard. Of course…that's what Mandy Mitchell wanted. She wasn't like most women who saw dollar signs and private jets and a life of luxury with him. She saw…Ezekiel, the kid she'd never noticed in high school.

What was it going to take to erase that lifelong first impression? Trust, first. "Absolutely a straightforward business arrangement," he assured her. "In fact, why don't we draw up a contract?"

Her eyes widened at that, and he could have sworn he saw a glimmer of horror. "A contract?"

"So you know I'm serious." He glanced around, reluctant to walk away and not get this close to her again for a while. His eyes landed on the roll of paper towels. "Here." Reaching over, he snagged one and tore it off.

"That's going to be your contract?"

"Legal and binding." He looked around again, and

she jutted her chin to the tiny desk built into the corner.

"There's a pen."

He turned, grabbed a felt-tipped pen from the cup, and laid the paper towel on the counter, smoothing it out as he bit off the pen cap and kept it between his teeth.

"I, Ezekiel Nicholas…" He scribbled the words, the ink bleeding on the soft paper towel. "Do agree to pay five thousand dollars to…" The pen cap garbled his words.

She slid it out from between his teeth. "Amanda Lockhart."

He grimaced. "You'll never be that to me." As he started to write the A, she put her hand over his.

"Okay, Mandy Mitchell. Only for you."

He hated that those words kicked his heart and her hand made him tense, so he nodded and looked down at the paper towel, turning the A into an M. "…Mandy Mitchell in exchange for…"

He hesitated again, and she got a little closer, so he could smell something citrus in her hair and feel the warmth of her. He continued writing. "In exchange for her appearance at social functions as my…" Then he looked at her, waiting for her to provide the descriptor.

"Pseudo? Imitation? Pretend? Fake?" She shrugged. "I don't know how else to say it."

"In math, any number that's the product of a real number and the square root of a negative one is referred to as imaginary. Would that work?"

She smiled. "Imaginary girlfriend it is."

On the contract, he finished the sentence. "…my imaginary girlfriend. Okay?" He searched her face, looking for humor in their little arrangement, but he didn't see anything but seriousness and, hell, a little fear. He hated the bastard who'd put that fear in her.

"No," she said softly. "You have to add that there can't be any..."

Sex. She might as well have spelled it out with her own marker. He turned back to the paper, his brain already seeking...loopholes. "We hereby swear that those services will not include..." His pen stilled as he waited for her to spell it out.

"You know," she said.

"I need a legal term."

"How about 'any activities that require the removal of clothes'?"

He lifted both brows, already seeing the loopholes and how to...get around, through, and under them. "Are you sure?"

"Well, I expect we'll have to, you know, hold hands and act like we're together in public. I mean, at least for the benefit of your mother and the Cinderellas at her ball."

He laughed softly. "You heard every word of what I said to her, didn't you?"

"Not on purpose," she said. "But, yeah, I picked up quite a bit."

He looked at her for a moment, enjoying the close contact, the chance to gaze into her eyes, and the softness he saw when she let her guard down. "Okay, then. Your words, your rules." On the paper, he wrote exactly what she'd said.

Any activities that require the removal of clothes.

"Is that ironclad enough for you?"

She leaned closer to read, her hair brushing his cheek as she did. Above her, he closed his eyes and took a silent breath of lemon and flowers, the desire for her as strong as the first day he'd seen her.

"That's good," she said.

He made two straight lines on the bottom, and then scratched his signature with little more than three strokes of the pen. He handed it to her, and she wrote very slowly, very clearly.

Mandy Mitchell. She smoothed the paper towel again. "I better be careful with this."

"I can put it in the safe in my villa," he said, reaching for it.

"Good idea." She turned, still trapped between him and the sink, and they looked at each other, a heartbeat of awkward followed by both of them laughing softly. "Should we shake?" she asked, holding out her hand.

"As long as our clothes stay on…" He took her hand and gave it a firm shake, then pulled her fingers to his mouth, dying for one more touch of his lips against her skin. "We're legal."

Her eyes shuttered as he pressed his mouth to her knuckles.

"So, when is the party?" she asked.

"The party isn't until Saturday. I'll arrange for a personal shopper from Naples to come here with samples of clothes for you to wear." At her look of surprise, he added, "I mean, if you're forced to keep them on, you might as well like what you're wearing, right?"

"Right. Is that how you shop? They come to you?"

"Now," he admitted with a laugh. But she still looked stunned and about to turn down the offer. "Mandy…" He took her chin and angled her face toward his. "There are some perks to being my girlfriend, even an imaginary one. Oh, I almost forgot." He picked up the check he'd set on the counter. "This is yours."

She eyed the check, then him, then the check again. "Thank you."

He slid it into her fingers, relaxed now. "It's a pleasure doing business with you, Mandy."

"Yeah, Zeke." She slipped away. "I'm sorry if I seem, well, odd to you. I hope you understand."

"You don't seem odd."

He followed her into the living room, getting the clear message she was walking him to the door. There, he added, "You seem like you've been hurt and you're protecting yourself."

She gave him a grateful smile, one that warmed her eyes and made him ache to take her in his arms. "I really appreciate you being so understanding." She stopped at the door and turned the handle to usher him out. "Then, I guess I'll see you Saturday."

Loophole number one. "No, not Saturday. Tomorrow. At six."

"Tomorrow?"

"I'm having dinner with a client." Again, her mouth opened with an "o" of disbelief. He fluttered the paper towel he was holding. "This doesn't specify that we're only going to be together for that party. I'm here for a week, so I've got an imaginary girlfriend for that week."

"But…"

"I'll follow the rules, Mandy," he promised. "And you'll enjoy a trip to Miami."

"Miami? That's a long drive."

"Oh, we're not driving. I have a helicopter chartered for six-thirty. We'll go a little early and swing over the Everglades."

"The Ever..." She let out a breathy laugh, all color draining from her face. "Oh...okay. I guess. I don't really love to fly."

"This is nothing like flying." He brushed her cheek as he walked out. "It'll be amazing. You'll see." It took everything in him not to kiss her, but he managed to get out the door without giving in.

He'd won round one. Mandy Mitchell was his girlfriend. He'd take care of the "imaginary" part in no time.

The day had started dreamy, moved into unbelievable, and right now? A nightmare.

Every bump, jolt, drop, and roll had Amanda holding tighter to Zeke, her gaze out the helicopter window. All the beauty below was lost, though, as Amanda imagined what it would feel like to die.

The burnished gold sunset behind them and the cobalt waters of the Atlantic ahead of them, even the bright strip of land she recognized as Miami Beach, were just a blur right now.

"Don't be scared." Zeke rubbed his thumb along the inside of Amanda's wrist, his finger warm and the pressure welcome, but neither enough to slow a heart that thumped with the same beat as the blades overhead.

She shook her head, and leaned closer to him, giving a quick look to the pilot, who could hear every word they said through the microphones attached to their headsets. Captain Davis already knew she was terrified, and that was embarrassing enough.

"It's not what I expected," she said, her voice muffled in the headsets that pressed around her ears and drowned out the more deafening sounds of the chopper. "Really, nothing today has been that way," she added.

The whole day had been amazing, though. Not at all what one would expect from the day after being fired. She'd met with the bank, an attorney, and even had had lunch with her friend Jenna, who used to work at Casa Blanca but now was second-in-command at a small housekeeping service in Naples. She'd learned so much and gotten so much closer to her dream that it was dizzying.

Not like this ride, however.

Then, when she'd gotten home, a stylist and personal shopper had showed up along with a wardrobe that a movie star would envy, and they'd dressed and made her up for tonight like she…well, like she was a star. Was that how rich people lived, she wondered as she smoothed the tangerine-colored silk of the high-low strapless dress they'd chosen. She crossed her legs to admire the strappy sandals…and caught Zeke admiring, too.

He made no effort to pretend otherwise, leaning closer and threading his fingers through her hair and brushing her bare shoulder. As he did, the helicopter took a fast fall, making Amanda let out a tiny shriek as she clutched his other hand, a damp palm pressed against his dry, cool one.

"Sorry about that, folks," the pilot said. "Getting a little gusty tonight. But on your left, you'll see our destination. So, not much longer now."

Except…they still had to get down. Amanda tamped

her growing fear; she'd always hated to fly, hated that she had no control, hated the fact that she simply didn't understand the physics of it…and this was like flying on steroids.

The pilot dropped them lower, giving them a chance to see the twilight glinting off the white sand of Miami Beach.

"That's Fisher Island," Zeke told her, using their joined hands to point to a triangular-shaped island at the lower tip of Miami Beach. "We're going to that house, on the eastern side."

She followed his gaze but didn't see a house, unless… "That's a house? It looks like a hotel."

Zeke laughed. "Garrett Flynn is a little extravagant. And Meredith, his wife, is an incredible hostess, so the estate is lavish."

Lavish was an understatement. Amanda forgot the helicopter horror for a moment, studying the waterfront property consisting of several red-topped Spanish-style structures situated around a center pool the size of a small lake, complete with a waterfall. A yacht and several smaller boats were moored at a long dock.

"Flynn's a venture capitalist," Zeke said, as if that explained the insane luxury.

"From the looks of it, a good one," she added. "Is that how you know him? Through business?"

"And we're in the same club in New York. Also, before he got married last year, he was on my softball team."

She couldn't imagine being young enough to be on a softball team and owning that estate. But then, look at the man next to her.

The chopper took another free fall, and the pilot tipped to the left, making Amanda seize up again. "Whoa," she whispered.

"Sorry again, folks," the pilot said into their ears. "We definitely are hitting some turbulence."

Zeke put a solid arm around her. "No need to worry. Captain Davis is the best in the business."

"Thank you, sir," the pilot said.

He slid Mandy's headset off her ear, pushing his microphone back so he could speak directly, and privately, to her. "We're almost there, Mandy," he whispered, the warmth of his breath and the genuine kindness in his voice sending chills over her. "Just relax."

She threw him a grateful glance, aware that the pilot might not hear Zeke's whispers, but he could hear her response. "I'm trying," she mouthed, her grip on his hand hard enough to dig her nails into his skin.

"Think about how much fun you're going to have tonight. It's a beautiful place, right on the water, and Flynn and Meredith are great people. I know they'll have a good crowd."

Her eyes flashed. "I thought it was a business meeting."

"I mix business and pleasure all the time."

She slid him a look and gave a sly smile of warning. Had he forgotten already that this was "strictly business"?

"Well, not all the time," he added, close enough to her ear that each word tickled. "You do remember that you're there as my girlfriend?"

"Imaginary," she reminded him.

"Folks, we'll be landing in a few minutes," the pilot

76

said. "But it's going to be a bumpy one, so hang on."

"Oh, great." Mandy tried to laugh but failed as her imagination went crazy with how bad "bumpy" could be.

"Stay calm," Zeke whispered, lifting her hand to his mouth to kiss the jitters away. It almost worked.

As they descended lower, the turbulence increased, forcing the pilot to make a wide turn and hover. She leaned over and looked out, the Atlantic Ocean far, far below.

"Helicopters crash," she said softly.

"Not this one," Zeke replied, reminding her that he could hear even her most private whispers. And so could Captain Davis. A strong bump jolted them into each other and elicited a soft cry from her.

The pilot was speaking softly to the Fisher Island helo control tower, the words "rough" and "turbulent" and "wind velocity" doing nothing to ease her fears. Zeke must have sensed that because he leaned forward and signaled to the pilot to give them a private channel. Instantly, the ground control communication ended, but she and Zeke could still talk to each other.

She wasn't sure if that was better or not, but at least the pilot wouldn't hear now how scared she was. She let her taut posture loosen slightly as Zeke repositioned his headset and mouthpiece to talk to her.

"I can distract you," he offered, taking both her hands in his and holding tight.

He could and he did. And that was almost more dangerous than the winds that buffeted them.

"Hey." He tugged her hands to turn her right to him. "Talk to me. It'll help."

"I can't talk." The headsets magnified the tension of

her words.

"Sure you can. You want to know about people you'll meet tonight?"

She nodded, trying to turn back to the window, but he wouldn't let her. She tried to think of something that would genuinely get her mind off the turbulence. "Tell me about your softball team. What's the name of it?"

"The Niners."

"'Cause there are nine on a baseball team?"

"No, because there are..." He hesitated, shaking his head. "It's kind of a joke."

"What's the joke?" she asked, keeping her voice steady despite the next rough bounce.

The chopper dropped hard, whipping to the right as it did. She let out a groan of fresh fear. "Please tell me something to get my mind off the fact that we're about to die."

He laughed softly. "We're not going to die."

"Niners, like it's a play on the 49ers?" she asked. "The football team?"

"No." He definitely seemed uncomfortable with the topic, and just as she was about to let it drop, he leaned closer and said, "It's a reference to zeroes."

Zeroes? They're all a bunch of zeroes? She shook her head, not understanding.

"In our net worth," he added.

A slight frown pulled as she visualized that many zeroes and then...holy shit. "Nine?" she asked, all the fear gone and replaced by astonishment.

That made him...a...she imagined a number with nine zeroes. "As in..." Her mouth formed a "b," but no sound came out.

Another shrug. "I told you, I've had some success."

"*Some* success?" She practically choked, the helicopter momentarily forgotten. "Wow. Really? Nine?"

He laughed, studying her. "You really didn't know that? It's pretty easy to find out with one Google search. The first story that comes up is from *Forbes*, calling me one of the top twenty most elig..." His voice trailed off, and the helicopter hit a welcome but rare smooth section of air.

Most eligible billionaires was what he was going to say, she assumed. "No," she replied. "I didn't Google you." Then her heart stopped. "Did you Google me?"

The helicopter jolted again, knocking them hard and turning her words into a soft shriek.

The pilot was too busy getting them down to even throw back an apology, so Zeke pulled her closer, but it didn't work. "Of course not."

But his words were lost as the whole chopper vibrated and rumbled, bouncing in the wind like a kid's toy on water.

"Oh, my God." She barely mouthed the words. "I'm sorry to be so scared. I hate this."

"Don't be sorry. But I promise, I travel like this all the time. This is really rare."

She nodded, biting her lip and holding his gaze. "I don't want to die before I start my business," she whispered.

"You're not going to die."

She closed her eyes without answering.

"Mandy." He pulled her into him, fighting the pressure of his seat belt to get closer and wrap her in his arms. "Don't be scared," he said. "Don't be..."

It wasn't working; she was shuddering. With one quick look to the pilot, he snapped his mouthpiece down and did the same to hers.

Just as they plunged another few feet, he kissed her. She moaned into his mouth but didn't move away because this...this felt so good. If she was going to die, it would be kissing this beautiful billionaire.

She grabbed his head and pulled him harder against her mouth. Taking the cue, he deepened the kiss, opening his lips, letting their tongues clash and collide.

He tasted like peppermint and safety, closing his hands over her face to hold her right where he wanted, each second of contact making the wind seem to die down. Or maybe she forgot to be afraid because this felt so good.

She took a breath, let out a soft sigh, and deepened the kiss. They stayed that way until they jolted one last time, hitting the concrete of Fisher Island Heliport.

"Uh, we made it, folks."

The pilot's voice, back in their ears, jolted them apart.

"Sorry for the rough ride."

She closed her eyes. "That wasn't rough," she whispered. "That was perfect."

Chapter Seven

Finally on solid ground, Amanda really tried to put that little tidbit of information on the back burner as Zeke ushered her to a private car, which took them around the island to the mind-boggling waterfront mansion owned by debonair Garrett Flynn and his vivacious and quite pregnant wife, Meredith. Still affected by the turbulence—and that kiss—Amanda managed not to swipe a damp palm over the couture dress before shaking their hands.

Instead, she took steadying breaths and tried not to ogle the surroundings as she was handed a crystal goblet of champagne, greeted by some of the other twenty or so guests, and introduced proudly by Zeke as his girlfriend, Mandy Mitchell.

His *imaginary* girlfriend.

Well, that made sense, because everything definitely had a fantasy-like feel to it. From the wall-to-wall aquarium stocked with sharks—real ones—in the living room to the multi-layered pool with at least fifteen canopied bed-like lounges around it, nothing seemed *real*. So it was fine to pretend to belong to the attentive man at her side as twilight descended over paradise and the first few sips of champagne took away Amanda's nerves.

But every once in a while, in the middle of light, breezy conversations with people who all looked like they'd stepped out of a Ralph Lauren ad, she'd glance up at Zeke, and he'd give her a smile that was very real.

After one conversation ended and that couple stepped away, Zeke and Amanda were alone, side by side, facing the deepening-blue ocean that grew darker as some evening clouds gathered.

"So, what do you think?" he asked softly, the question innocuous, but the tone was intimate.

"About?"

He didn't answer right away, but smiled. "The house? The party? Your boyfriend?"

The word did a really unholy thing to her insides. "The house is breathtaking. The party is exquisite. And the boyfriend..." Is breathtaking *and* exquisite. "Has really honed his social skills since Mimosa High."

He laughed. "You know you could totally wreck my reputation with that secret knowledge about what a loser I was in high school."

"Loser?" She scoffed at the word. "If so, you shook that label quite nicely."

"You're being kind," he said. "As far as the social skills, some networking comes with the job."

The job of being a billionaire. "Speaking of jobs, this isn't quite what I pictured when you said you had a business dinner you wanted me to attend." Amanda gestured toward the infinity pool and the yacht just beyond it, taking in the small crowd, harpist, and white-jacketed waiters. "I thought I'd be surrounded by stodgy old men in a dark restaurant where I'd be sitting next to you like an accessory while you planned to take over Wall Street."

"No stodgy old men or dark restaurants in business anymore," he explained. "And Wall Street takeovers are so last millennium. But you know what's most wrong with your picture?" He leaned closer, his hand secure and seductive on her shoulder, his mouth kissably close. "You could never be an accessory to any man."

The words sent a splash of white hot emotion into her stomach. Yes, she could. And she shouldn't let champagne, chiffon, or sharks let her forget it. "Not again," she said softly.

A frown pulled his brows together. "One of these days you'll have to tell me about this jerk you married."

Her whole body tightened. "One of these days, I will." She tried to inch away. "But not tonight. This is too beautiful and too much fun for ancient history. This is really…" So not the time and place for that particular confession. "Are all *your* houses like this one?"

"I'm more understated than Garrett. I have a nice place in the city, though, overlooking Central Park. And a really pretty Victorian in San Francisco with plenty of room if you want to come and visit California."

She let the invitation pass. *Pretend would end*, and she couldn't forget that.

"Flynn likes to flash his money," he said quickly, as though he'd read the look of discomfort on her face. "But he's much more settled down now that he's married and has a baby on the way. Much happier."

She couldn't help detecting a wistful note in his voice. "Is that what you want?"

He didn't answer right away. "Isn't that the American dream?" he finally asked.

She gave a disdainful, but soft, snort. "You're *living* the American dream, Zeke."

"Not entirely." The subtext in his voice couldn't be ignored this time. "Not like Garrett," he added.

"Garrett seems happy," she agreed. "But, trust me…" She looked hard at Zeke, wondering how honest she should be. Under the circumstances, not too open. "Marriage can be a nightmare."

He didn't flinch, his eyes reflecting the water beyond them as he gave her a questioning look. "Did he hurt you that bad, Mandy?"

Why sugarcoat it? "Yes."

"I'm sorry." He turned her so that they were facing each other, the breeze lifting her hair and the way he looked at her lifting her heart. "I'm sorry he broke you so badly."

Denial rose up, swift and certain. "I'm not broken. And, thanks to you, I am well on my way to complete independence, which is all I crave, ever." She lifted her glass in a toast, even though the champagne was nearly gone. "So thank you, Ezekiel Nicholas, for doing deals great and small, even with me."

He tapped his glass to hers. "Mandy." Never had anyone made her name sound so pretty. "I'm having a hard time."

Having a hard time breathing? Because that simple task was next to impossible for her right at this second, under the onslaught of this man's insane attention. "How so?"

He let his gaze fall to her mouth, his expression telling her he was remembering the kiss on the helicopter. Done to distract and calm her, it had had the opposite effect, making her focused on him and completely unnerved.

"I'm having a hard time keeping this imaginary."

A ribbon of heat twirled through her, but her body betrayed her with chills. "Ah, yes, the man who hates to lie." She tried to keep it light, but her voice was tight. "You're doing a good job of pretending, though. I'm sure every person at this gathering believes I'm your girlfriend. Not that I understand why they need to."

"So I'm not lying. Remember? The contract." With his free hand, he held her chin, lifting it slightly as if he were getting ready to kiss her again. And, God help her, she would kiss him right back. "I'm a man who honors a contract, no matter what it's written on. Ask any of my business associates in this room."

"Whoa, Nicholas. Please tell me this is your long-lost sister you've brought to meet me."

Zeke closed his eyes and broke into a wry smile. "Except this one," he said under his breath. "Don't ask this one *anything*." He turned, shaking his head, still smiling as he extended his hand. "I didn't know you were here, Becker."

"When Garrett Flynn sends his private jet, I board and fly where it takes me, because it's usually somewhere cool. Or hot. And speaking of hot..." He shook Zeke's hand but kept his dark, penetrating gaze on Amanda. "Hel*lo*." He positively drawled the word. Nearly as tall as Zeke and every bit as well-built, this man had a face that looked more rugged, less clean shaven, and raw.

"Mandy, this is Elliott Becker, who is best kept at arm's length. Becker, let me present Mandy Mitchell, who is *not* my sister and quite immune to your fake Texas twang and oversized, uh, ego."

Elliott's easy smile crinkled tanned skin and made his

midnight-black eyes dance with humor. "The twang isn't fake, darlin', and the ego isn't the only sizable thing on me. God, you're gorgeous. Ditch this human computer and marry me."

She laughed, instantly charmed. But Zeke speared him with a look. "She's too smart for you."

"Who isn't?" he joked, winking at Amanda. "I'm still amazed they let me on the team. I'm the dumbest third baseman ever."

Dumb as a fox, she suspected, if he was one of the Niners. "I doubt that."

Elliott reached for her glass. "Smart enough to know when a lady needs a drink." He put the glass under Zeke's nose. "Get with the program, Genius. Your girl's parched."

Zeke took the glass, giving him an amused glare. "Do your best, Becker. It won't work. She's mine."

"You can't blame a man for trying."

Zeke laughed. "No, I can't. Excuse me, Mandy."

He stepped away, and instantly the other man got a little closer, a scent of sandalwood adding to his allure. "Where did he find you?"

"High school," she said.

"No shit. Sweethearts?"

"Not exactly. We had longing eye contact across the cafeteria."

"Really? I pictured Zeke more of the lost-in-the-library type back then."

"You can't imagine." She gave him a slow smile, wanting to protect—and even improve—Zeke's reputation. "Every girl in school wanted him in the worst way." Wanted his GPA, so that wasn't a lie.

Both his eyebrows shot up. "Including you?"

"At the front of his line."

He made a little snort of surprise, which gave her a weird jolt of pleasure. "So where you been all these years?" he asked.

Married and held prisoner. She lifted a shoulder and kept the banter going. "Just waiting for him to sow his wild oats."

"Zeke? The brainiac? He's never been the biggest ladies' man on the team."

"How many of, uh, you guys are on this team?" There couldn't be too many Niners running around.

"Well, they have been dropping like flies lately. Flynn was one of the founders, but he's obviously off the team, and I'm a little worried about Lord Leo, who is rumored to have fallen flat on his face in love with a librarian, no less, up in someplace called Sanctuary Island."

There were lords on the team? "So if you move away, you're off the team?"

"Not exactly. If you—"

Another man sidled up next to Elliott, nudging him to the side. "You're out, Elliott. Zeke sent me over to pinch hit while he gets a drink."

What was this? Another god fallen down from Mount Niner? Amanda looked up at this newest arrival, meeting smoky gray eyes that looked…familiar. Recognizable. Even a little famous.

"I'm Nathaniel," he said with a picture-perfect smile.

"Nathaniel…Ivory." She managed to keep the stunned shock out of her voice, as a member of a family that some would call "American royalty" stood right in front of her—and not on the cover of some magazine. "Hello. I'm Amanda Lockhart, er, Mandy. Just call me Mandy."

Damn, her composure had slipped a little. But whose wouldn't? Naughty Nate, as the tabloids liked to call him, had hair a thousand shades of chestnut, a jaw like it was chiseled from marble, and that smile that every member of the Ivory family seemed to be blessed with. Along with…a reputation for trouble with a capital T.

"Mandy," he nodded, openly admiring her. "Well, now I understand why our poor Zeke is a puddle of nerves tonight."

"He is?" She glanced over her shoulder, seeing Zeke leaning against a bar, chatting with a woman. "He doesn't look nervous."

"Watch," Nathaniel said. "Give him three, two, one…there." As if on cue, Zeke turned from the woman and looked at Mandy, a little surprised to be caught by all of them.

The other two men lifted glasses to him in mock toasts, and Zeke shook his head, fighting a smile, before saying something to the woman.

"Mandy knew Zeke in high school," Elliott said, lifting one brow. "Apparently, Einstein was quite the catch back in his day."

Nathaniel let out a loud laugh. "Not a chance. He's a card-carrying nerd who, thanks to some very good friends, discovered that even rich men need to hit the gym."

"Oh, really?" She feigned surprise. "And here I recall they named a set of bleachers after him since he did the deed under them so many times after football games."

"He was on the football team?" Nathaniel choked.

"And not a virgin?" Elliott added.

She gave a broad smile, careful not to lie. "Trust me, a cheerleader never forgets."

She could feel Zeke coming up behind her. Maybe she could smell his cologne or sense the other two men shifting toward him, but his hand on her shoulder was no surprise. In fact, it was welcome.

"What are you telling these clowns?"

"I'm sharing what you were like in high school." She felt his hand tighten on her shoulder, a flash of disappointment darkening his eyes.

"Who knew you were Most Likely to Get Laid?" Elliott drawled, giving Zeke a playful punch.

Surprise flickered on his expression, then it slipped back to cool and calm as he pulled Amanda a little closer. "I don't like to brag."

"Your girlfriend is doing it for you," Nathaniel said.

"Are you, now?" He rubbed her arm affectionately. "And here I thought she never even noticed me back then."

She looked up at him, lost for a moment in the warmth and invitation in his eyes. "If that was the case, I was blind and stupid."

His eyes shuttered as if she'd kissed him, the compliment obviously going straight to his heart. He didn't reply, but they shared an achingly long look.

"Well, she sure as heck is noticing you now." Elliott put his glass up for a toast. "Let's make a bet on how soon we'll need a right fielder."

"Why would you need one?" Amanda asked.

The other two men fought a laugh, but Zeke looked serious. "Careful what you say, gentlemen. I don't want to scare her off."

"Why would I be scared?"

Elliott leaned closer. "We have a strict 'bachelors

only' rule on the Niners. Once you lose that status, you're off the team."

Oh, dear. Pretend really *did* have to end. She managed to keep her face expressionless.

Zeke, on the other hand, seemed completely relaxed at the implication, his hand slowly moving up and down her arm possessively. She wanted to hate the sensation, but, damn it, she didn't hate it at all. Still, she didn't look up at him, too terrified to see what she might read in his eyes.

There was no way they'd need a new right fielder because of her. She simply couldn't get in any deeper than she already was.

After dinner, the party moved inside as the breeze picked up and rain threatened. While Zeke and Mandy chatted with Meredith about the latest addition to the shark tank, Garrett joined them and wrapped a loving arm around his wife to whisper in her ear.

Zeke watched the exchange, aware of the tug of envy for what they shared. His friend had been lost and lonely a few years ago, bouncing from woman to woman and bed to bed. Then Meredith had appeared, and wham, Zeke had witnessed Garrett transform from playboy to peaceful.

Zeke had never been much of a player, though the women were available at every turn. That wasn't what he wanted. Under his possessive arm, he stroked Mandy's bare shoulder, the contact getting far too familiar, too good. Could she fill the hole in his heart? Did he dare give another woman a chance, after—

"Gotta steal Zeke for some business," Garrett said to the group.

Meredith reached for Mandy's hand. "I'll entertain your beautiful girlfriend, Zeke. Go talk shop with my husband."

"I'm fine," Mandy said, though he had to say there'd been a subtle shift in her demeanor since Nate and Elliott had made their stupid jokes about losing a right fielder. Nothing he could exactly pinpoint, but he didn't relish the idea of leaving her.

Still, he knew Garrett's invitation to the dinner party hadn't been strictly social, so he owed this time to his host. "I won't be long," he whispered, adding a kiss to her soft hair.

She glanced up and smiled, that wariness that had shown up earlier still taking her eyes from grass-green to the dark shade of a raw Colombian emerald.

"We'll be in the study with Nate and Elliott," Garrett told his wife. Then he gestured toward the window. "Looks like Mother Nature refused to cooperate with your plans for an after-dinner cruise."

Meredith waved her hand. "Can't control the weather. We're fine inside, but..." She gave another look at the sky. "I think some of you will not be getting in a helicopter tonight."

Zeke had already thought of that but hadn't suggested turning the evening into an overnight—not with Mandy so skittish. He let Garrett lead him away to the study before they could start that discussion.

In Garrett's oversized and over-masculine two-story

library, Elliott and Nate lounged, talking.

"We were just making friendly wagers," Nate said, as Zeke joined them in another leather chair.

"On what Garrett's latest insane scheme is?" Zeke asked, grinning at their host, who had a reputation for outrageous ideas. Obviously, they paid off, but it took balls of steel to do a deal with the guy. Zeke had done many, of course, all profitable.

"No, we're betting on how long until you're off the team."

He didn't answer, but Garrett brought over a bottle of port and gestured toward crystal glasses, eyeing Zeke. "She's a lovely young woman."

"She is that," he agreed.

"You sure she's legit?" Nate asked.

"Legit?" He scoffed at the word, using it to avoid confirmation or denial. "Coming from you, I suppose you're asking if she's got blue blood that can be traced to Plymouth Rock."

Nate angled his head in consent. "I never heard of Lockharts."

Had she introduced herself that way? Why did she insist on using that name? "That's a married name. She's divorced."

Elliott leaned forward. "I like her, Zeke, but you have to be careful."

In other words, watch out for money-grabbing gold-diggers. As if he didn't know that. "I am."

Garrett had his phone out, tapping the screen, almost as if he weren't listening. "I'd like to be sure she isn't going to break our boy's heart."

The other two men laughed softly, but Zeke put his hand on Garrett's phone, pushing it down. "No need to run a search on her. We're safe in that department." Except, he knew for damn sure his heart wasn't safe at all. It might already be a lost cause. "And if not?" he added, digging for a certain kind of casual he didn't exactly feel. "I don't like to play things safe, as you all know."

"Good," Garrett said, settling into the fourth chair. "Because I have one hell of a dangerous proposal, and you are the three to make it happen."

Happy that the conversation was off Mandy, Zeke shifted his attention to business. "Let's hear it."

Garrett folded his arms and looked from one to the other. "I've heard each of you on different occasions proclaim that you'd like to own a professional baseball team."

He had all of them instantly. They didn't bother to share a look; they'd talked about this over post-game beers many times. Elliott, Nate, and Zeke shared a love of the sport and deep desire to be team owners.

"Oh, baby." Nate leaned forward and put his elbows on his knees. "You got that right. The only problem is there isn't one in the entire country interested in selling right now. Trust me, we've looked."

"What about starting one?" Garrett asked.

"Too much legwork," Elliott said.

"And years before you have a competitive team," Nate added. Of course, that would matter to Nate, who didn't know the definition of defeat.

"Not to mention that buying a Major League team would take more money than the three of us would part with that easily," Zeke said, already doing the math in his head and coming up with…astronomical.

But Garrett ignored the arguments. "I didn't say

Major League." They all started to speak, but Garrett waved them off. "Hear me out. I'm talking about a privately owned minor league baseball team."

"None of those for sale right now, either," Nate said.

"You can buy equity stakes, though," Zeke told them. "I've looked into a couple of teams. Quite profitable. But..." He gave a shrug. "Not the game we're interested in, right?"

The other two men agreed.

"I'm not talking about an equity deal," Garrett said. "I'm talking about starting a minor league team from the ground up. Including building a stadium that can be used for MLB spring training, which would pretty much pay for itself in a few years."

All three men looked at each other, Elliott's eyes the widest. "Build a stadium?" The real estate mogul in him looked fascinated. "I like that idea."

"It needs to be in Florida," Garrett said. "Because I'm here now more than I'm anywhere else, but it can't be the east coast of the state because of spring-training travel logistics. The big teams have almost all moved to the Gulf Coast. We need to find a location, do a land deal, get the stadium built, and start recruiting players. I've got more friends involved, but I want you to be the core team. I know your hearts are into this."

Zeke knew where he stood. The closest thing he'd ever gotten to playing ball as a kid was running algorithms on statistics. He played softball now, and each game made him want to be more involved with baseball. And not as a spectator; that wasn't good enough for him. He'd always known that someday he'd buy a team.

"I love this idea," he said, unable to hide his

enthusiasm. "I'm all in."

Garrett beamed as Nate lifted his port glass. "I'm interested if I can have a hands-on role. I don't want to be an angel investor."

"Same here," Elliott said. "What's our next step?"

Garrett beamed, obviously expecting this response. "Lawyers, of course," he said. "And we have to scout a location. We can hire someone to do that because I don't have time to drive up and down the state, but I do have a few locations I think could sustain a medium-to-small stadium."

"I'm over on the west coast all week," Zeke said, already loving the realization that the project would have him back in Florida—with Mandy—on a regular basis. "Give me your list, and I can check out some sites. Then we'll turn it over to professionals—"

"Like me," Elliott said. "I think I've proved I can close the deal on a good piece of land."

Considering that Becker had made his fortune at twenty-five by buying an innocuous property in New England that happened to have two billion dollars' worth of solid Goshen stone on it, he certainly had the qualifications there.

"You can have that job, Becker," Zeke agreed. "And when we get close to building—"

"I'll handle that," Nate offered. His family money meant he never had to work, but Nate had proved himself to have excellent project management skills.

"Gentlemen." Garrett stood and raised his glass, and they all followed suit. "Let's play ball."

They toasted just as a thunderclap shook the house and rain splattered on the window. "Didn't you come by helo?" Nate asked.

Zeke lifted his glass. "But not going back that way," he

said.

"Not tonight," Garrett agreed. "You and Mandy can stay here, of course. I'll get a guest suite prepared." He took a moment to lift his brows. "One room or two?"

Zeke didn't hesitate a second. "One." Yes, they had a contract…but he could definitely find some loopholes tonight.

Chapter Eight

There never was a moment to say no. The party ended, the weather escalated, the overnight guests were ushered to their rooms. Or room, as the case may be. Of course, Amanda and Zeke weren't flying back to Florida's west coast in a storm, and it seemed crazy to go to a hotel when they were in a house this size, but...

Amanda swallowed against a dry throat as she entered the softly lit guest suite on the second floor and heard Zeke behind her, saying good night to their hosts, giving her a minute to get situated.

She looked around, admiring a floor-to-ceiling fireplace in the middle of a cozy sitting area. French doors lined one wall, looking out to a wide veranda, only partially covered by an awning, the rest designed for private sunbathing. Tonight, however, rain blurred what must have been a million-dollar view beyond that. Large double doors opened to a bathroom the size of a small country, and another set led to a walk-in closet. In the middle of the room...the elephant—an ultra-king-size bed covered in silk pillows and draped in sheer curtains.

One great big mistake just waiting to be made.

"Your dress is going to be a mess."

She wheeled around at Zeke's voice, catching him as he closed the door and locked it behind him. "Excuse me?"

"From sleeping in it." He took a few steps closer, fighting a smile. "I mean, if you're going by the letter of our law."

The contract that said no clothes would ever come off. She'd thought that would be enough to keep them out of bed. Of course, she hadn't planned to be trapped in a suite overnight with him.

"Then you're going to be uncomfortable, too." She gestured toward his dress shirt and trousers. "Maybe you should have thought of that when you told Garrett we only needed one room."

She gave him a minute to deny that, but he lifted a shoulder. "I didn't want to leave you."

Points for honesty. And the ability to turn her lower half into a pool of lust with so few words and one hot look.

"Anyway, if you read that contract closely, it doesn't specify *whose* clothes," he said. "I can take mine off."

Oh, please don't do that. She'd never manage to keep her hands off him.

"Or you can take yours off."

She narrowed her eyes and crossed her arms. "You know damn well what I meant when I put that line in our deal. All clothes stay on. All hands kept to ourselves. All…stuff…is off-limits."

"Stuff? Is that what the kids are calling it these days?" In three long strides, he closed the space between them, his eyes bright.

"Whatever you call it, I was trying to keep us from a

Secrets on the Sand

situation like…" She angled her head toward the bed. "This."

"Yeah, that." Eyeing the bed, he sidestepped her and lifted one of the sheer drapes off a hook to slip it a few inches across the canopy. "Nice bed. You could sleep in here without clothes on, and I wouldn't even see you." He fingered the fabric. "Although, this is pretty sheer. But if we turn the lights off, you're safe."

"I know I'm safe," she admitted. He'd never lay a hand on her if she didn't want him to. The problem was…look at him. *That* was the problem. His hair was a little messy from the wind outside, his collar open, his sleeves rolled up to expose strong forearms.

He sat on the bed, the flouncy comforter puffing up around his legs. "I'll sleep on the floor."

"Don't be silly."

"I bet the tub's huge."

She smiled. "Safe bet, but no."

He fell back and spread his arms across the bed. "I'll fit on that settee."

"I doubt that."

He patted a pillow as if inviting her. "There's a chaise on the balcony. I don't mind rain."

"Saying one thing, doing another." Laughing softly, she took a few tentative steps closer, unable to resist the sheer pleasure of looking at him spread out on the bed. His hair dark against the shades of cream and ivory, his arms open as if she could…climb on. His eyes closed, and she ventured closer, quietly inhaling the clean scent of him.

"Is that a yes?" he asked when she didn't answer.

But she crept one step closer, careful not to touch him. His eyes stayed firmly shut, and his chest rose and

99

fell with slow, even breaths. If she hadn't known better, she'd have thought he was asleep, and that gave her the confidence to get so close she could see his eyelashes brush against his cheek and the shadow of his whiskers. She let her gaze drift lower, counting a few stray hairs that peeked from the top button of the shirt pulled over well-developed pecs.

He still didn't move, so she kept looking, at his narrow waist and hips, and the rise...oh.

He snagged her hand so fast she gasped as he yanked her onto the bed next to him with a slow, easy laugh, curling his whole body around her. "You're staring at me, Mandy Mitchell."

She tried to deny it, but that came out as a soft catch of her throat at the pressure of his body next to hers. The sweet, sweet pressure.

"I guess you owe me some staring." His voice was gruff. "I stared at you enough."

"In high school?"

"Tonight." He eased her even closer, lining up their bodies on the bed. It felt so natural and right. But it wasn't, and she couldn't forget that. "Didn't you feel it?"

"Mmmm." She closed her eyes and nodded, ignoring the warning bells to enjoy the solid man next to her. "I did."

"And you know what I was thinking?" With one finger, he traced her profile, brushing lightly over and over across her lower lip.

"About that contract you signed?" She tipped her head to the side to catch his smile. He was so close, she could see the different shades of blue in his eyes, the silver rims, the dark pupils. Eyes that held hers, then searched her face as if he were looking for the perfect place to…

"Yep," he whispered. "And all the ways I can get around the terms of our deal."

She didn't breathe, slowly realizing that her hands were locked on to his upper arms, the rock-hard muscle pressing into her palms. His leg rested over her thighs, and that rise she'd noticed?

Rising against her hip.

Everything in her—every single female cell in her body—ached for him. She wanted to turn, to press, to feel his hard maleness right where she wanted it. "You can't…" Her voice was barely a breath.

He pressed his lips against her temple. "I can." And he…was.

"But you can't…"

He feathered kisses down her cheek, making his way to her mouth. "There's nothing in that contract about…" He grazed his tongue over her lower lip, making everything tight and hot and painfully aware of every inch of his body hardening against her. "Kissing."

"But I can't…"

"You don't have to do a thing, Mandy." His fingertips brushed along her jaw and chin, the touch so gentle it could have been air. Unable to stop herself, she felt her back bow, her face lift, her throat exposed to his touch. He ran his thumb over the skin, circling the dip between her collarbones, trailing a hot line lower and lower.

"I have to breathe. And think. And stay sane." She turned her face to him. "All of which I am right now forgetting how to do."

His hand flattened over her breastbone, a strong,

huge, masculine hand with enough pressure to make her want to beg for him to…keep going. He leaned over her, his mouth barely an inch from hers.

"You're breathing." He kissed her gently. "What did you think of that?"

"Nice."

"See? You're thinking. What was the last thing you said you forgot? Oh, sanity." He lowered his head and nestled under her throat, sucking softly at her skin. His hand dragged down over the silk of her dress as his erection grew mighty against her. "Sanity is overrated."

She wanted to laugh, but nothing was funny. Nothing was real. Just the touch of his hand and the heat of his body and the taste of his lips. "Zeke…"

He lifted his head and looked at her, his eyes dark with arousal. "You want to break the contract?" he asked hopefully.

She shook her head, biting her mouth closed to keep the "yes" from popping out.

He slowly moved his hand, her breast under his palm now, shooting sparks between her legs and making her want to scream. Instead, she squeezed his biceps with all the strength she had, and he slowly eased himself further on top of her. "Zeke."

"What do you want, Mandy?" He pressed harder, making everything hot and dizzy and so, so needy.

This. She wanted this. And, oh, that. And…oh, that gentle kiss. His mouth was like warm water, his hands sure but kind, his legs wrapping around her…he rocked into her, the unforgiving might of his erection shocking her.

"It's been so…long." She rose and fell against him,

completely unable to stop the waves. "But I'm…" How could she even say the word?

He rose an inch. "Please don't be scared of me, Mandy."

She wasn't, but she was scared of this. Of how close this was getting to something she'd absolutely sworn she'd never do. His serious tone made her open her eyes and look right into his. She should tell him the truth. She should tell him what she'd had to fight and how ugly this beautiful act had become for her.

But that would ruin everything.

"I'm not scared of you," she said softly. "Just men like you."

Very slowly, he lifted his hand from her breast and took all the pressure of his body to the side, releasing her. Instantly, she was cold and lonely and achy in a completely different way.

"I'm not like anyone you've ever met," he said simply. "And if keeping that contract will prove it to you, well, then…" He inched her bodice higher, getting her strapless dress right back in place. "I can wait."

She didn't answer, searching his face, knowing he had to feel her heart thump the way she felt his. A billionaire with a good heart? Was this even possible? Could she trust him?

"You can wait?" she asked.

"What's another few days after twelve years?" He kissed her cheek and inched her toward the pillow. "Sleep with me. Just sleep."

She could do that. The realization that she most certainly could do that, and it wouldn't be wrong or stupid or anything but amazing washed over her as cool as the rain pounding on the balcony.

"Yes," she sighed, rolling into his arms. "I can sleep with you."

Hours later, Amanda woke up sweating and tangled. Without thinking, she turned to the man she'd fallen asleep next to, ready to make a joke about how her dress—her three-thousand-dollar designer dress—was wrapped around her legs.

But the pillow next to her was empty. Sitting up, Amanda blinked into the darkness. Cool air ruffled the drapes shrouding the bed, the sound of steady rain loud enough for her to know the French doors were opened. Thunder rumbled in the distance.

They'd fallen asleep on top of the covers, but at some point, Zeke had pulled the comforter down and covered her with a sheet.

She threw that off and pushed back the sheer drape, peering into the darkness toward the balcony. It was hard to see, but it looked like he stood leaning against the railing, face up to the sky, rain pouring on him.

He needed to be alone. Needed to do his...waiting.

Her heart folded as she remembered the words he'd whispered to her.

I can wait.

But could he wait forever? She let out a long, slow breath of sadness and frustration. She should tell him now. She should tell him what he was getting into and how...unavailable she was emotionally and physically and every other way a man might want her.

How would he take it? She barely knew him, but she had a sense that he was a man of honor. He was also a man who got what he wanted. A man who could tear a paper-towel contract in two with one sexy, talented hand. He could lick a contract apart, kiss it to pieces, make a mockery of...*legalities*.

And he seemed to want more than sex, or was that her dreaming and fantasizing that he truly was the perfect man?

Another long, low rumble of thunder rolled over the Atlantic Ocean, echoing in the room. Her entire being longed to bring him back to bed. But she couldn't—she *shouldn't*—do that.

She slipped her feet to the floor, the sheer dress damp from sweat and discomfort. The bodice squeezed her top, the material stuck to her legs. Her fingers brushed something cool and crisp, and she lifted Zeke's shirt, which he'd left on the bed.

Without a second's hesitation, she slipped out of the dress, wearing nothing but a tiny silk thong. The room lit with distant lightning, enough for Amanda to see Zeke's silhouette standing on the wide balcony, the marbled section protruding out further than the overhang, rain drenching him.

She stuck her arms in his shirt, buttoning a few buttons and standing so that it fell to her bare thighs. Taking a breath, she calmed herself and walked slowly toward the storm outside, which could only be a little more dangerous than the one raging inside her.

She had to do something. She had to.

Water sluiced down Zeke's bare chest, dousing his hair, soaking his skin, and plastering the pants that still hung unbuttoned to his body. Mother Nature's cold shower was doing its job, and he didn't have to go into the bathroom and run water to keep his erection at bay.

Around three, he'd awakened, a curvy, sexy, soft, sweet woman in his arms, her breath against his cheek, her sleepy sighs as intoxicating as the port he'd had in Garrett's library. With each moment, he'd grown hotter, harder, and more desperate to touch her.

He'd stroked her arm, let their feet brush, and listened to the music of a moan she'd never know she'd let out. If he'd touched Mandy, she would have responded. Their bodies were meant for each other, ready for the inevitable.

But the pain in her eyes after their kiss had told him the ice-cold reality that some heartless bastard had slashed her heart. No, he couldn't do anything that would—

He shuddered as arms wrapped around his waist, stunning him with warmth and invitation.

"What are you doing out here, Ezekiel?"

Her voice was musical, gentle against the distant backdrop of thunder.

"Solving a quadratic equation."

He felt her laugh. "What a geek."

"It's that or break the contract."

She scraped her fingers over his chest. "You already did. This is not your shirt."

He put his hand on her arm, recognizing the feel of familiar fabric, already wet from the downpour. "No, but this is."

"I borrowed. Is that okay under our contract?"

Mandy was in his shirt. The thought shot fire into his

groin, taking him back to the state he'd tried for the last twenty minutes to drown. "No," he said, the roughness in his voice surprising him. "Not okay."

In one easy move, he pulled her around his body, getting her right in front of him against the railing. She was rain-soaked already, the water battering her hair and pouring down her face. But she looked up at him, undaunted by a little smeared makeup and a storm.

"The rules didn't say whose clothes we had to wear," she whispered. "And it was the closest thing to you in that empty bed."

Her words slayed him, punctuated by a flash of lightning in the distance. The light was just enough to highlight his wet dress shirt flattened against her body, molded to her form, the shape of her breasts visible, the points of her nipples like gumdrops he needed to taste.

Instinctively, he leaned her back so more rain poured over her. She dropped her head and let the water cover her face and slide down her neck and into the shirt.

How had this happened? What lottery had he won? What good deed had he done? What karmic retribution put her in his arms? "Mandy Mitchell."

She smiled, her back still arched, pressing her against him. "I really never thought I'd be called that again in this life," she said.

Still holding her with one steady arm, he lost the battle not to touch her hardened nipples. He flattened his hand over the shirt, right over her heart, and slowly, easily, gradually dragged his palm until he cupped her breast.

She gasped softly, straightening, her eyes wide. He braced himself for the word "no" or that look that said sex terrified her. But her expression was soft, her jaw slack, her eyes dark with arousal.

A loud shot of thunder made her startle and suck in a breath, coming closer.

"All those nights, Mandy," he whispered into her dripping wet hair.

"All what nights?"

He thumbed her nipple, gratified by the hard, relentless point under his fingertip. "All those nights I'd sit in my room and solve equations and make graphs and torture my brain with mathematics…" He unbuttoned the top button, easily able to reach into the shirt and caress her breast.

For a minute, he couldn't talk, his whole brain flatlined by the perfection of her skin and the slope of her woman's body.

"But then I would think about you." His cock underscored the sentiment, growing harder against her belly.

She smiled, either because of the words or what she felt. "What did you think about, Ezekiel?"

"These." He squeezed her breast. "This." Soft, sweet, tender woman filled every sense as he brushed her lips with his. "And…" He slid his hand down to the bottom of the shirt, sliding easily between her legs, finding sweet, soft, soaked silk, the sexiness of it jolting him. "Of course, this."

She moaned as he stroked her panties and found a sweet spot.

"And what did you do?" she asked.

He wanted to laugh at the question, but he wasn't capable of anything but feeling her buckle a little under his touch. "Not calculus."

"Did you…" She wiped her hands down his chest, over his abs, lower to his already open pants, a question in her eyes.

He closed his eyes and hissed when her fingertip made contact with him, the slight touch injecting more blood to an already engorged hard-on. The rain was useless now, doing nothing but making this even sexier. "I did," he admitted. He buried his face in her hair, nestling into her neck, fighting the urge to howl and slam himself into her fist.

She moaned, clearly turned on by the thought. Pulling her in, he kissed her, tasting rain and the remnants of lip gloss, tasting sex and desire. "I want you, Mandy," he murmured as he broke the kiss. "Here, there, anywhere you'll have me. I want to be inside you. I want to make love to you."

The lightning answered for him, the shock of light catching unmitigated fear in her eyes.

There was no doubt about it. "Sex scares you," he said flatly.

She didn't answer, looking down, the distant rumble like an echo of her pain. "It does more than scare me," she said softly. "I...can't. I may never...again. I just can't."

Then he knew. All the comments about powerful men, her hesitation about sex, her assumption that everything between a man and a woman caused...pain.

She didn't say a word, the rain rolling over her cheeks like tears he knew with certainty she'd shed a million times. "He hurt you."

Her eyes shuttered. "I told you he did."

"No, he physically hurt you."

She didn't answer, biting her lip, looking down in shame.

"Tell me."

She shook her head.

"Please, Mandy. Did he…" God, he couldn't say the word. It made him recoil, a testosterone-induced rage bubbling through him. "If he hurt you, wherever he is, whoever he is, I'll kill him."

He could see her eyes fill despite the rain. "No, you can't. And that's not…please, Zeke. I can't talk about it."

"You should talk about it," he urged. "Let someone share your anger."

She shook her head again. "I'm past anger and, honestly, I didn't come out here to talk about that." Her fingers brushed his abs again, but the fire was gone.

Until she got over this—until she talked and healed—he wasn't going to have her. Not the way he wanted.

Far-off thunder rolled, and rain splattered around them, chilly now and not nearly as seductive as it had been a minute ago. No, until this pain was gone from her heart, every time they kissed and touched, some asshole came into the room with them.

He might want Mandy in every way a man could want a woman, but before they could share that, he had to at least try to help her forget the guy who'd wrecked her. Sighing, he put his arm around her. "Come in with me."

"I can't go to bed," she said, and he understood what she meant.

"I have a better idea."

Chapter Nine

Zeke brought Amanda towels and wrapped her in them, then sent her into the bathroom where she found a thick velour robe. She stayed in there a few minutes, corralling her composure, toweling off her hair, then staring in the mirror to see herself through Zeke's eyes.

But all she saw was...Doug Lockhart's wife. A shadow of the woman she could have been, and certainly not the woman Zeke thought she was.

She closed her eyes and released a pained sigh. She couldn't go the rest of her life alone, could she? But anything else meant...

A shudder passed through her whole body. She wanted him. Really, truly felt the desire that she'd long ago thought Doug had killed. But there it was, alive and sparking in every nerve ending in her body.

Oh, it had been so long since she'd made love to a man who cared about her feelings. In the early days of their marriage, Doug had, but then...things had escalated.

If he hurt you, wherever he is, whoever he is, I'll kill him.

Well, good luck finding him.

It would never get to that point. She couldn't let it, even if she did give in to her body's urges. In a week, Zeke would be gone. Pretend would end. She'd start her business, and he'd go back to his life in New York, and this would be nothing but a lovely interlude that made her feel beautiful again.

Holding that thought, she opened the door to find a fire raging in the fireplace and Zeke on one knee, adjusting the glass enclosure around the flames.

He was still bare-chested but must have found a pair of sleep pants. In the firelight, the muscles and cuts of his bare chest looked like an artist had painted them.

"Wow." Amanda ventured closer. "I'm impressed."

"Don't be. All I did was find the switch and turn on a gas fireplace." He stood, his body on full display, the drawstring around his waist loose enough so the pants fell over narrow hips, revealing more of his masculine form. "And I found some basic necessities in the armoire there. I should have known our hosts would provide sleepwear."

She pulled the robe a little tighter, more for protection than reluctance to give up its warmth for some flimsy nightgown. "They thought of everything."

"C'mere," he said, reaching for her hand. "Unless you want to go back to sleep."

She shook her head and walked closer, where he'd laid their comforter on the floor between a small sofa and the fire. The French doors were ajar, so she could still hear the sound of rain and thunder.

"The wet bar's stocked," he said. "You want anything?"

She considered that but then shook her head. "Too early for coffee and too late for wine."

"That magic hour of four AM." He took her hand. "Let's enjoy the fire, and maybe you'll fall back to sleep."

Doubtful, but the offer was too good to fight, so she let him guide her to the floor, fluffing the down around them, making a soft bed. He leaned against the sofa, facing the fire, and she naturally—so, so naturally—curled against his chest and let him wrap an arm around her.

Silent for a moment, he stroked her hair.

"I don't trust many people," he said, the low baritone of his voice as soothing as the thunder outside.

Grateful he was initiating the shared revelations, she snuggled closer.

"I would imagine," she said, staring into the dancing flames, "that when you are as successful and wealthy as you are, lots of people are out to use you."

He made a small grunt of agreement in his throat, his fingers threading her hair slowly, circling one damp strand.

"I'm always stunned by how many fakes there are in the world," he finally said.

The words hit low and hard, making her close her eyes while he continued.

"I guess because most of my life, I've really lived in and around numbers. Before those numbers translated to money, I knew who and what I could count on. But as the years went by, and I made more and more, I discovered that it is almost impossible to sift genuine people from phonies."

"You have to trust your judgment," she said.

"Funny thing about judgment. Mine seems to be in excellent working order when it comes to finance and business. I can smell a good investment, and my gut instinct is rarely wrong when sitting across the conference room table from a potential business partner."

She waited, knowing there had to be a "but" to this confession.

"But with women?" He gave a wry chuckle. "Man, I suck in that department."

"I find that hard to believe, Zeke. You're gorgeous, you're charming, you're genuine, and you're…"

"Loaded," he finished for her.

"I wasn't going to be that crass."

He shrugged, moving one sizable shoulder under her head. "I am. It's great, don't get me wrong. Money buys freedom and houses and four-million-dollar baseball jerseys and a hell of a lot of security. I suppose, if I so choose, it could buy me companionship."

Something dark in his tone made her look up. "They say it doesn't buy happiness."

He cupped her cheek, holding her face in his hand with such a gentle touch it made her eyes sting. "They're right."

"Aren't you happy, Zeke?"

He didn't answer, and her heart slipped a little. He stroked her cheek and met her gaze with one full of hurt and promise.

"Maybe you need…someone…" But not her. This was pretend…and pretend would end. It *had* to.

"Now you sound like my mother."

"Maybe she's right. Maybe you should…" She swallowed and rooted around for the right way to say this. "Maybe you should give some of those girls she's bringing to the party a chance."

He looked at her like she'd lost her mind, and then resumed his hair twirling and cheek caressing, their legs stretched out in front of them, his body stone still.

"I don't want one of those girls."

An icy cold fear tiptoed up her spine. Because she couldn't be what he was looking for. She couldn't.

"Have you ever given anyone a real chance?" she asked. "Surely you've met someone who you trusted."

He didn't respond, and she started to move to see his reaction, but he tensed his arm and kept her where she was, gathering up a handful of hair and bringing it to his nose to sniff. "You smell like rain."

"Mmm." She nestled closer, drawn to his warmth and body. "Good subject change."

"I'm not...okay. Yeah. I got hurt." He snorted softly, as if to say that was an understatement.

"I'm sorry to hear that." She gave him a second to continue, but he didn't. "How long ago?"

"Couple of years." Another sarcastic snort. "Three years and three months, seventeen days."

"Wow." She sat up this time. "Must have been serious if you remember the date."

"Well, I'm a math guy," he said quickly, and then he gave a shake of his head, as if he were trying to erase that. "Everyone remembers their wedding date, Mandy."

She opened her mouth, then closed it, letting the heartbreak in his voice settle over her. "Oh, no. Really?"

"Technically, rehearsal dinner."

She inched back. "She broke up with you at your rehearsal dinner? Was she crazy?"

He laughed. "I'm going to take that as a compliment."

"As you should. What kind of lunatic would leave a man like you?"

His eyes tapered into icy blue slits, zeroing in on her with enough intensity to send chills over her whole body. "Someday, Mandy Mitchell, I'm going to hold you to that."

Only he wasn't being playful. And if she wasn't careful, she would have herself in way, way too deep. But, honestly, the man was attractive, rich, and had a heart of gold. "What was wrong with this woman?" she asked.

"Apparently, everything, but I was too blind to see." He shook his head, pulling her back into him and drawing the comforter over their legs. "You want to hear the whole story?"

"Every gory detail. I've got all night."

"It's not that long. Or gory. We were at the rehearsal dinner, a banquet for family and friends at the Waldorf, and she got a call." He paused for a minute, as though traveling through time to remember.

"I could tell it was urgent and upsetting because she left the table in a rush and was gone...a long time." His fingers stilled on her hair. "I was worried about her, of course, so I went to check on her and finally found her..."

"Oh, no. She wasn't..." Images of finding his fiancée in the middle of a tryst flashed in her mind.

"No, she was sobbing. Absolutely bawling her eyes out in an empty meeting room at the end of the hall."

Amanda sat up. "What happened? Cold feet?"

"She was still in love with her *other boyfriend*." His voice grew tight. "And he had broken up with her."

"What the *what*?"

"No kidding. She'd been seeing someone for months, a married guy." His voice went flat—absolutely dead from an old pain. "She thought they'd stay together while we got married, and eventually they'd both get divorced, and she'd walked away with money because chump, moron, trusting guy that I am, we had no prenup."

"Oh, God." And Amanda's heart folded in half, stabbing her chest. No prenup. He'd trusted someone that much. "That had to hurt."

"I made it out safely, but, bottom line, I blame myself."

"Why?"

"Because I didn't see through her. I let lust and love and what I wanted more than anything—a partner in life—put blinders on me. She never loved me. She told me that night, all weepy and sobbing. She never loved me and…" He trailed off. "Man, I must sound like a loser."

"No, not at all." Her voice sounded thick in her throat, making it hard to talk. "You gave your heart and trusted and…" Heat crawled up through her as his words replayed. *What I wanted more than anything—a partner in life.*

What she wouldn't give to be that woman.

The thought stunned her, making her instinctively pull away.

"Hey," he said instantly, drawing her right back. "It's your turn."

No, her turn had come and gone, sadly. And now…knowing without a doubt what he wanted? Now she really should tell him everything.

"I did the same thing, Zeke. Only I married him, and

it took about seven years to realize that he never loved me, either. And there was a prenup, not at all in my favor. You're lucky you didn't have to go through that kind of pain."

He turned his face to press his mouth against her palm. "I don't think it has to be painful. Not love and not…any part of being together."

She knew exactly what he was referring to. She could tell him that much, right? "You've already figured out the gist of it."

"Sort of." He took her hand and pulled them both down to lie next to each other. "But since I told you my story, you have to tell me yours."

She let him line up their bodies with him on his back and her head on his shoulder, their legs entwined. They sank into the fluffy down, and he wrapped them tighter together. The rain had slowed to a drizzle, and the thunder had quieted, and the only sound was the soft hiss of the gas fireplace and the steady thump of her pulse against her throat.

Waiting for that to slow to a normal rate, she didn't talk, but let their breathing even out and match, her fingers on his chest, unable to resist touching him.

"He was a control freak," she finally said. "In every aspect of life."

"What does he do?"

Now? Who knew? "Commercial real estate." She flattened her hand and enjoyed the steady beat of Zeke's surprisingly dear and trusting heart. "He was very good at it, too. Well, when the market was strong, I mean. But I met him my senior year in college, and he was older by almost ten years and so…impressive. He seemed like the perfect husband. I really didn't have any great career dreams, to be honest. I wanted to be a great wife, do volunteer work, have some kids, be happy. I could lie and say I was ambitious, but I wasn't. Ironically, I'm more ambitious now."

"And were you happy?"

"For a while. Before we got around to kids, though, I had a sense that things weren't...perfect. Work was stressful, and the market was bad, and that made him..." Mean. "Rough."

He puffed out a disgusted breath. "He hit you?"

"No, he never hit me. He didn't beat me or ever make me scared for my safety. I wouldn't have stayed with him, I swear. When I say he was rough, I mean..." She swallowed, then took a deep breath. "Sex. He liked things...not tender." She almost laughed at the understatement. "Let's just say he had a domineering streak that really got, um, exaggerated in the bedroom."

Under her fingers, she felt his muscles tense and heart rate increase. "I take it that didn't, um, do it for you."

"Nope, not my style," she said softly, slowly. "I didn't want to do what he wanted to do." She closed her eyes, washed with the degrading memories. The truth rose up, ready to come out. She should tell him...everything. But something stopped her. Fear, remorse, shame, the knowledge that this had to end one way or another so why make admissions that would only haunt her and hurt him?

"Everything needs to be mutual," he said. "Whatever people do together, it has to be mutual."

"Well, it wasn't. So, eventually, we did nothing and he did whatever he did somewhere else. Of course, I filed for divorce."

"You're smart. You got out. Mandy, I admire your guts."

A chain of guilt snagged her heart, squeezing her chest. "It didn't take that much guts. But..." She swallowed the rest, absolutely unable to say the words.

"But what?"

"Well, I guess I feel kind of dumb, too. I signed the world's most horrific prenup, and now I'm..." She looked up at him and smiled. "Now I'm a maid."

"Not for long," he reminded her. "You'll be a business owner."

She patted his chest and nodded. "Thank you, Zeke."

"Hey, I'm happy to help you out."

"I mean, thank you for this. For holding me and talking to me. For not trying to... I mean, I was..." Ready to fall into bed with him. "Not sure how this would go."

He pulled her up closer, brushing a kiss on her temple, wiping away more damage with one kiss than he could ever realize. "I'd never hurt you, Mandy."

"I know."

"No, you don't," he whispered. "But I'll prove it to you. And once you're sure, once you're absolutely one hundred percent sure, we'll make love."

She closed her eyes and lifted her face, accepting the sweetest, softest, most beautiful kiss she'd ever had. "I'll never be—"

"Yes, you will." He feathered another kiss on her cheek, and her temple, and her ear. "You will be sure and ready and free. And the only tears you'll shed will be from pleasure and joy."

For a long time, Mandy just stared at the fire, both of them perfectly still until Zeke fell asleep in exactly that position. She watched him slumber, drank in the sunrise, and somehow managed to fight the tears as his last words played over in her head.

She might be sure. She might be ready. But she'd never be free. Not the way he wanted her to be. And that was the saddest thing she ever knew because sometime in the last few hours, this had ceased to be "pretend." But it still had to end.

Chapter Ten

Amanda couldn't breathe. Her heart pounded so hard she could hear each beat in her ears, and both of her palms sweat so much she had to turn them over to get some air on her skin. And she was shaking.

But Lacey Walker didn't seem to notice any of that as she turned the last page of the proposal.

"I'm impressed, Amanda," she said, finally looking up. "Simple, smart, incredibly efficient. I know I didn't give you much time."

Next to none, in fact. Amanda had called Lacey the day before to ask for a meeting, certain she'd be pushed back a week or more. But Lacey herself had called back almost immediately and invited Amanda to come in bright and early the next morning with her proposal.

Which wasn't ready. But thanks to Zeke, who'd stayed at Amanda's house until three that morning helping her put a plan together, she'd arrived here at nine, ready for Mimosa Maids to be considered for the outsourcing. They'd laughed, they'd argued, they'd finished, and somehow, they'd kept true to the letter of their contract. Clothes stayed on, even during a heated goodnight kiss.

A kiss that was going to lead to—

"But you wouldn't do that, would you, Amanda?"

She might. For three days, she'd been getting closer. She blinked at Lacey, digging for a suitably vague answer to cover her wandering mind. There wasn't one. "I'm sorry, Lacey, I'm nervous this morning and had about two hours' sleep."

Lacey broke into an easy smile. "I love that this means so much to you. I know the feeling."

She was counting on that. "My plans are a lot smaller than building a resort."

"Trust me, my plans were small, too." Lacey tossed back some curls with a laugh. "Then I met the architect, and his ideas were much bigger than mine." She held up her left hand to show a gold wedding band. "Much bigger."

Amanda's already pounding heart kicked up a notch just thinking about that, taking her back to the mantra that had put her to sleep the last few nights. *Pretend has to end. Pretend has to end.*

After his father's surprise party, Zeke would head back to New York, and his visits to Mimosa Key would be so infrequent, he'd surely forget her. Would she forget him?

She'd have to.

"My question is about the staffing. A big part of J&T's plan is to hire existing staff we have now and dedicate them to Casa Blanca. Are you prepared to do that?"

"There are several staff members I'd like to interview and consider, and I may hire new as well. I'm not afraid of working here every day until we have a fully trained housekeeping staff."

She nodded, considering that. "I like that. I know Jared is planning to move Tori into the office, and she won't be training staff." She sighed, shaking her head. "I need to give this some thought, Amanda, but I'm very intrigued by your ideas. Especially this Mega-Green cleaning line, which you've managed to make cost effective. Others promise similar things, but the fees for environmentally friendly products are sky-high."

Because Zeke owned a stake in the chemical development firm looking for beta testers of the new product line, she'd been able to get an amazing price on "green cleaners."

"I'm excited about that, too," Amanda said.

Lacey fluttered through the pages again, slowing on a spreadsheet and graph Zeke had created, nodding slowly. "Yes, this is quite an impressive piece of work." She closed the binder with a snap. "I'll be making a decision shortly."

"If there's anything else I can do, Lacey, just let—"

"Yes, there is."

Amanda leaned forward, ready for whatever she suggested. A test run, another interview, more numbers. "Anything."

"Accept my apology," Lacey said softly.

Didn't see that coming. "It's fine, Lacey. You're running a business."

"Mr. Nicholas came and personally spoke on your behalf."

She nodded, knowing he'd done that from the first night he showed up at her house with five thousand dollars in his pocket.

"I shouldn't have assumed the worst and fired you."

"I'm not a business owner, yet," she added with a

quick smile. "But I imagine you have to daily weigh what's best for your company versus what's best for your employees. I don't blame you for making that decision. In fact, I'm glad you did. It motivated me."

"To find the money, yes. How did you do that, by the way?"

"Creative financing," she said, confident that was no lie.

Lacey's smile was rueful enough that Amanda suggested she knew more than she was letting on. "Give me a few days, and I'll get back to you."

Outside of Lacey's office, Amanda took a minute to lean against the wall and close her eyes with a sigh of relief. This was all so close now. She started to head to the back door, then checked herself. She wasn't in uniform; in fact, she'd decided to wear a simple, but crazy expensive, polka dot dress the personal shopper had left when she'd delivered clothes for the surprise party. Right now, there was no reason to avoid the lobby, which was a much faster way out.

Opening the door that took her behind the front desk, she froze at the sight of Tori Drake clicking away on one of the computers. That wasn't unusual; the head housekeeper of the day often used the front computers to monitor checkouts to get the rooms cleaned while they were unoccupied.

But Amanda really didn't want a run-in with her now. She moved quickly, hoping Tori wouldn't notice her.

"What are you doing here?" The icy demand made Amanda freeze and swallow a curse.

She turned and smiled. "Seeing old friends."

The other woman's gaze dropped over the dress, her

lip curling slightly. "You've been banned from the property."

Not true. "Sorry, but you don't own the place."

"But I'm about to own housekeeping, and if you think you can come slinking around for your old job, you can—"

"Mandy!"

They both turned to see Zeke strolling across the lobby, his light, loose, linen shirt accentuating his body, his blue eyes locked on Amanda like she was his personal target. He had one hand behind his back and a very sexy smile on his face.

"Well, well, well," Tori ground out under her breath. "It's your favorite guest."

Amanda slipped out from behind the desk to get away from Tori and closer to Zeke.

"How did it go?" he asked, still not noticing Tori.

She nodded. "Good. It was—"

He brought his arm around and presented her with a single long-stemmed red rose. "I'd have brought champagne, but I figure after last night we both need coffee and rest before the party tonight."

She took the rose, pulling it to her nose to sniff but gave him a warning look, whispering, "Be careful what you say."

He looked past her, and she could have sworn she saw his lightning-fast brain compute the whole situation. "Excuse me for a second," he said softly, stepping away to the desk. "Ma'am?"

Tori gave him a sultry smile. "Yes?"

"My villa is ready for cleaning. My girlfriend and I will be out for the day. We'd like fresh sheets and champagne chilled by four. Will that be a problem?"

Her smile drooped like whipped cream thrown against the wall. "Of course not."

"Thank you." Then he turned to Amanda and put his arm around her. "Let's go, Gorgeous."

As he hugged her close to his side, Amanda looked up. "Why did you do that?"

"Never liked that girl in high school. She made fun of me."

On the way out, Amanda couldn't resist one look over her shoulder, expecting to see daggers in Tori's eyes. But that very second, Lacey stepped out of the management suite and asked Tori to come into her office.

It was almost midnight when the last of the non-family guests finally left the country club. The band was packing up, the waiters were cleaning, and Mom and Dad were hugging some old friends at the door. It was time; Zeke was ready to make his announcement, but he had to be extremely careful who heard what he had to tell them.

Nothing would be public for a while, but he was ready to tell his family the news. And Mandy, of course. He hoped she'd be as happy as he was.

"I guess she's lost her touch after all." Jerry sidled up next to Zeke at the bar, gesturing toward their mother with his glass. "The liedar is broken."

Zeke threw a look at his brother. "What makes you say that?" Had Mom figured out their ruse? He sure as hell hoped Violet hadn't cornered her older son to complain that the younger one wasn't really dating the girl he'd brought.

"You couldn't tell?" Jerry choked a laugh. "Dad wasn't surprised in the least when they walked in."

"I thought he was," Zeke said. "And Mom thought he was, which was all that mattered."

Jerry still shook his head. "He's known for weeks and that whole jaw-dropping, stuttering, and tears? He's been practicing that for days."

"And Mom couldn't tell? Impossible."

"I'm telling you. Her liedar must have been tied to hormones, and those are gone now." Jerry grinned, flashing his easy white smile and crinkling eyes as blue as the set that stared at Zeke in the mirror every morning. "Unless she's just so happy to see you in love that all internal systems went on the blink."

In love? Was his infatuation with Mandy that obvious? He glanced at the dinner table where Jerry's wife and Mandy were laughing, the connection between the two women easy and natural from the beginning. Everyone liked her, of course. Even Mom. Mandy had absolutely charmed Mom, of course, reminding him with a whisper during one particularly nice slow dance that she was only doing her job as his imaginary girlfriend.

Except, not one second of this evening had felt "imaginary" to him. And when he made his announcement, all that pretend business would be over. Anticipation and something that felt as close to a happiness more raw than he could ever remember rolled through him.

"So tell me more about Mandy," Jerry said, interrupting Zeke's thoughts. "You met her at the resort, you said. I'd love to hear about that."

"No, I would." From behind Zeke, their mother stepped between her sons. "I've been dying to get you alone, Ezekiel." She slipped her arm through his. "You see, I have so many mothers and daughters angry at me right now, I'll be needing you to write a lot of checks to charities to make up for the empty promises I made."

He smiled down at her. "I told you not to go to that trouble, Mom."

"Are you *really* dating her?" she asked. "Because I know she's divorced and works as a housekeeper, but—"

"Those details don't make her who she is," he said defensively.

"I know that," Mom insisted. "I'm trying to tell you I like her. She's charming and pretty and..." Mom sneaked a look at the table. "Maybe she won't insist on going to work so much that she can't have a baby."

On the other side, Jerry gave a soft grunt. "Mom, Laura's the—"

"I know, I know." She waved a dismissive hand. "I'm putting my hopes on Ezekiel now. Please tell me this is not some short-term fling of the week."

He easily met her eyes, unafraid of liedar, whether or not it had disappeared with menopause. Because this wasn't a lie. "It's not a short-term fling."

She scrutinized his face with the same distrusting expression she'd wear when he'd tell her he'd gone to bed at eleven but really stayed up until four on his computer. "How can I be sure?"

Just that moment, Mandy looked over her shoulder and caught his eye, sending that same happiness zinging through him. And only a little trepidation. She should be happy about his news.

It was time to find out.

He set his glass on the bar and put an arm around his brother and mother. "I'll prove it right now. Let's get Dad and go sit down. I have something I want to share with you."

His mother's eyes widened. "Really? Oh, my God, really?"

He didn't answer as he walked her to the table and Jerry went to retrieve Dad. In a moment, they gathered together, Jerry and Laura, his wife of six years, Mom and Dad, and Zeke and Mandy. It felt so natural, like she belonged in his family.

"I have some news," he said without preamble.

Jerry and Laura shared a look, and Dad launched a snow-white brow to the north, and Mom beamed like a Christmas tree.

"I love news," she said.

Next to him, Mandy gave him an uncertain look. "Good news?" she asked.

"Fantastic news." He gestured them all a little closer, despite the fact that only the wait staff was in hearing distance. But wait staff could talk. "This is family confidential. You cannot breathe a word."

"Why not?" his father demanded. "If it's good news, we share it."

"No," Zeke said. "We have to handle the announcement very carefully, because this could be a delicate situation."

Mom's gaze zeroed in on Mandy's stomach. "How delicate?"

"No, no." Zeke waved her off with a laugh, putting an easy hand on Mandy's back and feeling her stiffen at the implication. "Different kind of good news."

Mom pressed her hands together under her chin, nearly jumping out of her skin. "Oh, this is so exciting."

"Yes, it is," Zeke agreed. "This is something I've wanted for a long time." All five of them looked at him expectantly, and he breathed the words quietly, "My own baseball team."

"*What*?" Mom's and Dad's simultaneous questions shot like a bullet across the table.

"Really?" Jerry leaned forward. "You're buying a team?"

He could have sworn he felt Mandy sigh with relief.

"Starting one from scratch," he said, reaching under the table to find her hand, hoping she liked the important part of his news. "My buddy Garrett Flynn proposed the idea to a few of our friends, and I've spent some time this week doing some site selection for a location to build a facility for a minor league team and to possibly use for Major League spring training."

"Is that what you've been doing?" Mandy asked.

"I wanted you to come, but you were so busy with your own business, I couldn't take you."

Mom's face had slowly faded to abject disappointment. "That's it? That's your news?"

"No. That's not the best part." He squeezed Mandy's hand. "I've found a location after spending a lot of this week searching up and down the west coast of the state." He turned to Mandy and met her gaze, hoping to see joy in those bright green eyes. "I found about a hundred and fifty acres of undeveloped land right on Mimosa Key in the northeast corner of Barefoot Bay. Which will get me back down here…all the time."

He felt her gasp more than heard it, nothing but shock and…well, not joy in her eyes.

"Northeast Barefoot?" Dad leaned forward before Zeke could interpret Mandy's reaction. "There's nothing up there but an old goat farm."

"That man died, I heard," his mother said. "Cardinale. His granddaughter's been living there since he passed. Is she selling?"

"She's going to," he said confidently, turning to Mandy. "Once we put Elliott Becker on the job."

But she didn't laugh or even reply, her face pale, her eyes still registering disbelief. Inside, all the excitement numbed as he realized...she wasn't happy.

Jerry and Laura were throwing questions at him, Dad was adding to the melee, and Mom looked torn between disappointed and hopeful. But all that didn't really matter because he'd expected Mandy to look thrilled, but she was anything but.

In fact, she barely smiled.

Chapter Eleven

The low-grade panic that had started when Zeke shared his news bubbled up in Amanda's chest, squeezing everything until she couldn't breathe. Her heart walloped her ribs, and every once in a while, she got a little dizzy. Somehow, she managed to chatter with everyone else and hold Zeke's hand as they all left the country club to wait for their cars.

This shouldn't have happened. She had no right and no desire to fall for someone again. That wasn't the plan! That wasn't independence, plus she—

"Here's our car," Zeke said as the limo pulled up to the country club entrance. He guided her into the back seat, gave one last wave to family members then slid in next to her. The car smelled rich, like clean leather, the lights barely on, the windows black.

"My girl is upset." Zeke eased them both to the wide back seat, folding her in his arms. "Isn't she?"

She let out the breath she'd been holding for a long, long time. "This would be a hell of a lot easier if you'd please be an asshole rich guy I'd like to punch."

He grinned.

"And it would help if your family weren't so nice."

He laughed.

"And if you wouldn't do things that make me want to…"

"Want to what?"

Break every rule for you. "Kiss you."

"What did I do that made you want to kiss me?"

"Pretty much just standing, sitting, being, and breathing."

He let out a soft moan and pulled her into his lap. "The party's over, sweetheart."

It sure was.

"Now we are free to…" He dragged her dress up to her thighs, and then eased one of her legs over him, so she was straddling and facing him. "Break the contract."

"I'm not fr—"

He stopped her with a kiss, pulling her with both hands on her shoulders, situating her right over a mighty erection that pressed hard against her bottom, her pearly pink dress balled up between them.

As he broke the mouth-to-mouth contact, he slid his hands down, over the neckline and onto her breasts, making it impossible to talk or think. She had to *feel*. His hands erased everything.

He rocked once, making her gasp. She dropped her head back, the blood rushing through her doing exactly what she wanted it to do—clearing her head of any thoughts. Of any rationalizations. Of any truths or fears or problems this was going to lead to.

Instead, she felt the burn of his lips on her skin, the heat of his fingers as they wandered up her thighs, cupping her bottom, and caressing the most tender spot between her legs.

"Zeke…" She couldn't breathe, her body coiled tight

with how much she wanted his fingers on every bit of her skin, his mouth everywhere else, and his whole manhood deep, deep inside her. Just thinking of that made her roll against his hard-on, earning a grunt of pain and pleasure and an intensified sucking against her neck.

The rumble of the causeway under the tires told her they were almost home, and when they got there…

"I want to make love to you," he rasped into their kiss. "I want every inch of you, Mandy Mitchell." He slipped a finger into her wet panties, deep enough to know without a doubt that she wanted the same thing. "I will be so gentle," he promised.

The words tore her heart out. "I know you will, but…"

"Don't be scared, honey. I will go so slowly." He stroked her with his thumb. "So soft and sweet and easy." Sparks ignited between her legs, fueled by the seductive words.

She could barely nod, her breath so twisted in her lungs, fighting the orgasm that already threatened. One more second, one more caress, one more promise, and she'd be gone.

"This is…wrong."

"It's going to be all right," he assured her. "We're going to tear that contract to shreds. Along with this dress."

"No, I mean—"

The limo came to a stop in the driveway of his villa. She eased off him, straightening her dress and hair, trying to get her breath. He could tear that paper-towel contract and this dress, and it wouldn't change anything. She was…who she was.

And she could never be his.

Except…maybe this one night, before he left. One night, one time, one sweet, sweet night…she could be his. Doug couldn't steal everything from her. He couldn't take away this one night.

* * *

Zeke had Mandy in his arms before the lights of the limo disappeared, scooping her right off the ground and carrying her up to the door, her laughter like music as she dropped her head back.

"What are you doing?"

"Sweeping you off your feet. And, shit, the key's in my pocket."

She reached her hand between them, going for his pocket but landing on his throbbing hard-on instead. He hissed. "Don't make me drop you, Mandy."

She laughed again, giving him a squeeze, then finding her way into the pocket to produce the card key. "Voilà!" She held it up, and he positioned her so she could unlock the door, and he pushed them in.

"Are you going to put me down?"

"On the bed." He took her straight down the hall to the bedroom, where the efficient staff had followed his secret instructions and left about two dozen hurricane-style candles burning around the whole room.

"Zeke!" she exclaimed as he set her on the bed, kneeling over her. "This is so romantic."

"I wanted our first time to be perfect for you, Mandy." He slowly lowered himself to the bed. "As perfect as you are."

Her eyes fluttered in acknowledgment of that, each breath she took slow and strained.

"I never want to hurt you." He traced a line along her cheek and jaw, sliding up to her parted lips.

She whispered something he didn't catch. Pretend end? "What was that?"

Her eyes darkened under a frown. "Zeke, this was only supposed to be for a week."

He kissed her softly, tracing his lips to her ears. "What is this 'supposed to' you speak of?"

She shuddered a little, and he kissed her with every ounce of tenderness a man with a raging boner could manage, letting her warm to the intimacy and relax in his arms. But she seemed more tense.

"Deep breaths, Mandy. I'm not going to hurt you."

A fine sheen of sweat glistened on her shoulders, so he kissed it, tasting salt and perfume and sweet, sweet Mandy. He lifted her body enough to unzip her dress in the back.

"Zeke, I really shouldn't…"

"Shhh." He feathered kisses over her breastbone, tugging the strapless dress lower and lower until her breasts were revealed. He dipped his head to kiss one and caress the other, making her gasp and arch her back.

"Oh, my…"

He ran his tongue over her nipple, loving the hard bud and sweet taste, sucking hard enough to make a noise. Blood rushed in his head, amazing him that there was any left there, considering how much had flowed to his lower half.

Still, he fought to hold back, easing that dress down, watching her chest rise and fall and seem to fight a losing battle.

Her head moved back and forth, almost as if she was saying…no. He paused for a moment, so hyperaware of her fears, stilling his hands.

"Zeke, we…can't."

"We can," he whispered, inching his way up to kiss her mouth and talk to her. "We really can."

"But…there's this paper…"

He laughed softly. "You're going to hold me to that contract?"

For a minute, her whole body stilled, and then she looked at him. "What good is a contract if you ignore it?"

Was she serious? "How about I burn it?"

"Zeke, I have to… there's something—"

A soft tap on the outside door cut her off and made him frown. "Did you hear that?"

"Housekeeping!"

Her eyes widened. "It's Tori!"

"Shit." He pushed off the bed. "Don't move. I'll take care of her."

"Zeke, wait." She grabbed his arm. "I have to tell you something. It's important. I have to—"

"Housekeeping!" She was *inside*!

He let out a disgusted grunt. "Does she think this is how to keep guests happy? Hold your thought, I'll be right back."

Why would she come in, he wondered as he marched down the hall. The wall safe where he kept valuables was hidden in the dining area, but she'd know that. She wouldn't know the combination, though. He turned into the living room and found her putting something on the coffee table.

"What the hell do you want?"

She straightened, unafraid or even surprised to see him. "I've left something for you, sir."

At this hour? "What is it?"

"Oh, a special gift from housekeeping." She gave a

tight smile. "Hope the sheets were clean enough for you and Mrs. Lockhart."

She pivoted and walked to the door, yanking it open and disappearing into the dark. What the hell? He grabbed the envelope but didn't bother to open it, too eager to get back to Mandy.

On his way out, he stepped into the dining room and opened the cabinet where the safe was, tapping in the digital combination he'd set. Deep in the safe, he found the paper towel they'd used to write their contract.

It was time to put those candle flames to good use.

In the bedroom door, he paused, blinking into the flickering light when he didn't see Mandy on the bed. Or anywhere. "Mandy?" He checked the bathroom, but the door was open and the lights were off.

Where did she go? The French doors to the patio were open, and he stepped closer, seeing her immediately, walking by the pool, her arms wrapped around herself as she whispered, like she was...

Talking to herself? Like she was...practicing what she wanted to say to him?

His heart nearly collapsed. She'd had so much pain, so many fears. But he didn't care. He'd conquer every one of them. He'd beat anything and anyone down to have her in his arms, afraid of nothing.

He started to go outside but decided to give her a minute. Let her gather her thoughts and make her speech.

Instead, he dropped into a chair in the sitting area and ripped open the envelope that had his name on it. He unfolded the paper inside, frowning at the legal document as he tipped it to read by candlelight.

"What is this?" He turned the paper closer to the

flame and squinted at the tiny print, a seal at the top, and names...he recognized.

A slow, icy chill wormed through his body as the words almost made sense. All of the words. Even the maid's parting shot.

Hope the sheets were clean enough for you and Mrs. Lockhart.

"Zeke."

He looked up, surprised to find Mandy a foot away, her arms still crossed, her face streaked with tears. He blinked at her.

"I'm still married." The words were barely a breath of air.

He let the paper flutter to the floor. "I know."

Chapter Twelve

The thing that buckled Amanda's knees wasn't that he knew her secret…it was how stricken he looked. He stared at her with vacant eyes, the slightest frown of pain and disbelief pulling his brow, his whole body hunched in a self-protective posture.

She knelt in front of him. "I was trying to tell you."

"Now?" The word ground out like one syllable of agony. "How about, oh, a week ago?"

"I didn't think it mattered a week ago."

"You didn't—"

"This wasn't real, Zeke!"

He straightened at the force of her words, leaning back, looking at her…as if for the first time. With all that awe and joy and interest and attraction she'd been basking in for the past week wiped away, replaced by raw hurt.

That was the worst part. "The fact is, I'm legally bound—"

"To your husband." Anger darkened his words.

"To a nondisclosure agreement that is part of the world's most horrific prenup. I really cannot talk about my husband or where he is, but that's easy enough because I don't know where he is."

He stared at her, the only thing moving on his body were the tips of his fingers, which slowly dug into the armrests of the chair with the same pressure she imagined they'd like to dig into her chest and rip out her heart right now.

And that was the only reason she had to break the agreement and risk the truth.

"He's a criminal," she said softly.

He still didn't speak, searching her face and waiting for more.

"He took millions of dollars for a fake real estate investment and to develop this big park and residential area in Tampa. He swindled five investors out of about ten million dollars and claimed to have a bank guarantee from somewhere in Switzerland and a commitment from some fund in New York. It was all lies. He thought he could float money, finish one project and start another..." She closed her eyes, almost relieved to be saying this to someone other than a federal investigator.

"We were divorced, for all intents and purposes. I'd moved out, had a plan, even had a little bit of money. All the paperwork was done, I was walking away with nothing, but he had one more paper to sign." Her voice cracked. "He refused and disappeared that night."

His fingers pressed harder. "Why wasn't he arrested?"

"They can't find him, and he won't come back into this country. Because we weren't divorced, I had to turn over whatever money I could to the federal government. My name is on many of his documents, and I'm trying, dollar by dollar, to pay people back, and the investigators insist I use my married name so anyone he owes money to can find me."

"They don't know where he is?" He sounded incredulous.

"I've heard he's in Croatia, and Australia, and Singapore, and the latest sighting was Hong Kong. There's some extradition glitch with criminals there, so he might think he's safe. I used every dime I had left to pay for a private investigator. All I want him to do is sign the piece of paper and let me be free of this marriage and this debt and the weight of…my past. I want to be free."

She dropped down to sit on the floor, the pressure of the story almost too much for her. Zeke made no effort to reach out to her or even soften the look on his face.

"In my prenuptial agreement, there is a line that says I can't reveal anything I know about his business, so I'm in a really bad position."

"That's void if he's a criminal."

"One would think, and I certainly told the investigators everything I knew, but…I'm afraid if I break that agreement, I'll never get him to sign that decree. I keep hoping he will meet a woman and *want* to sign it, but…"

She'd never imagined *she'd* meet someone. Someone so good and right and real that he made everything she thought she knew about powerful men seem wrong.

Quiet for a long time, he finally swallowed and nodded. "If you really wanted to, you could find him."

The allegation stung. "Trust me, I want to." Now, more than ever.

"Do you? Or are you protecting yourself, Mandy? Do

you want to be certain you don't have to take another risk so you stay...married?"

"No," she answered without hesitation.

"Really? Because you crave independence, but you don't go after it."

She let out a soft, shuddering sigh. "I don't know how," she admitted.

Finally, he nodded. "I understand."

"You do?" She barely understood, so how could he?

"I wish you'd told me, but—"

"I thought this was strictly business, Zeke."

He closed his eyes, like the words were a direct hit to his heart. "That's where I made my first mistake." He pushed up, stepping around her. "But I won't make a second."

The words sounded cold and harsh and...deserved. She inched back as he walked away.

"Would you like me to drive you home?" he asked.

For some reason, that question did her in. The dismissal of it. The finality. And, no, she didn't want him to drive her home. She couldn't bear to be alone tonight.

"I'll sleep upstairs, if you don't mind."

"I don't mind."

Tears burned behind her lids. Pushing up, she stood and watched him walk across the room, not sure what to do. Then he stood very still, as if he was having an internal debate.

Turn around, Zeke. Turn around and forgive me. Turn around and take me in your arms and tell me that we'll figure this out.

He didn't move.

"Zeke..."

"I have to make a phone call," he said, the tone still utterly...icy.

She deserved that. Without a word, she walked out and padded up the stairs, closing the door in the guest room but not locking it. Because she still hoped he'd come up to her.

An hour passed, and she was still alone. Still in a frothy pink dress he'd bought for her, alone in a guest room she'd cleaned for him not a week ago.

She rolled up on the bed, pulled the comforter over her and finally, fitfully fell asleep. When she opened her eyes, the very first whisper of dawn touched the morning sky beyond the plantation shutters she hadn't bothered to close.

And she was still alone.

Pushing up from the bed, she wiped sleep away and waited for the realization that she'd had a very bad dream. But it was no dream. She opened the door and peered into the dark, and then tiptoed down the stairs, sensing something different about the villa. Emptiness.

"Oh, no, please." The words slipped out from behind her fingers, as if she could contain the pain she knew she was about to endure.

She went straight down the hall to the master bedroom and into the open door. The room was empty, the rose petals and candles out of sight, the Egyptian cotton sheets stripped off the bed.

Any sign that Zeke Nicholas had been a guest was gone.

Amanda wasted no time doing what she had to do. At eight-thirty that morning, she was waiting outside Lacey's office, hoping to be the first meeting of the day for the Casa Blanca owner.

As Lacey came around the corner, she slowed her step and gave a warm smile in greeting. "Amanda, I love your ambition," she said with a laugh. "You aren't going to wait for me to make this decision, are you?"

Amanda swallowed hard, smoothing her hands over her dress. "Actually, I've come to withdraw my proposal, Lacey."

Amber-brown eyes widened in surprise and disappointment. "Why?"

She'd never say. "And I also am here to ask if you'd consider letting me have my old job back."

Lacey let out a low sigh, clearly not thrilled with either request. "Come on in, let's talk."

But there would be no talking—not openly. Just some begging. She had to repay Zeke somehow. She'd spent two thousand of his loan starting her business, and she wanted to pay back every dime, as quickly as possible. This was the most expeditious way she could think of.

In the office, Amanda perched on the edge of the guest chair, while Lacey followed her in, hooked her bag on the back of the door and closed it with a sharp snap. "What happened?" she asked before she even sat down.

"My...my..." She hadn't expected Lacey to ask. "My financing fell through," she finally said. And that was kind of the truth.

"Yes, I saw his name on the morning checkout list."

Amanda closed her eyes, unable to meet Lacey's gaze. "Don't judge," she whispered.

Lacey surprised her with a sharp laugh. "Judge? You

are talking to the wrong woman. Honey, I have been there and done that and have the baby to prove it doesn't always go south when a man helps you out. So, what happened?" she repeated.

"I...he...we..." She laughed at her pathetic stuttering, taking a deep breath to find some composure. "It's a long story."

"I like long stories, but give me the abbreviated version. He wanted more than you're willing to give?"

A warm blush rose up. "Am I that transparent?"

"No, he was. When he came to our house, the guy was already half gone. But I know you're a private woman, so I haven't been able to read your take." She leaned forward, dropping her chin on her knuckles. "He's a catch. Great-looking, wealthy, caring. What's his fatal flaw?"

"He doesn't have one," Amanda admitted glumly. "I do."

"And it is?"

She nodded. "You're right about me. Private. And so's my answer to that question."

Lacey grew quiet, considering a reply. "You know what meeting my husband made me realize?" She lifted her hand as if to say, *Don't bother, it's a rhetorical question*. Then she leaned closer, narrowing her eyes. "When it's real, anything is possible."

Her chest squeezed. "This wasn't real." It was, in fact, imaginary.

"Then better you learn that now before you make any lifelong mistakes, right?"

Right. "I guess."

"I was going to give you the business."

Damn, damn, *damn*. "I can't do it, Lacey. I have to

pay back his loan. Otherwise…" *I'm no better than my husband, the swindler.* "I shouldn't have taken it in the first place."

"Well, that's a shame, because I loved your proposal. And I have some serious issues with Tori and Jared. For the time being, I'll continue to manage housekeeping through the resort and revisit the outsourcing at a later date. Maybe by then you can re-bid for the job."

"Maybe." But she sounded about as confident as she felt. Like, maybe pigs could fly. "But right now, I need an income. Can I work for you again?"

Before she answered, her phone rang. "Hang on," she said, lifting the receiver on her desk. "Lacey Walker."

As Lacey listened to her caller, Amanda waited, her heart still hammering from making the request.

"She did *what*?" Lacey's voice rose as she stood, sounding astonished by whatever news had just been delivered. "Take her passkey and send her to my office."

Lacey clicked off the call and remained standing, looking down at Amanda. "When he checked out, Mr. Nicholas reported that Tori broke into his villa at one in the morning. Do you know if that's true?"

"She used her passkey. I was there."

Lacey puffed out a breath and fell back into her chair. "I'm letting her go."

Ding, dong, the witch is dead. Small consolation now.

"But then I have some scheduling problems."

"I'll help you," Amanda said, leaning forward. "I'll work anytime, any job, anything."

Lacey's smile was slow and kind of sad as she shook her head. "You really need to have your own business. I'll take you up on that offer and give you triple time if you work the reunion I'm having in a week. I'm really short that night, and it will definitely count as overtime, since working the reunion means you'll miss enjoying it."

Amanda frowned. "What reunion?"

"Oh, you weren't here for the last all-staff meeting. I had a great idea for some local marketing. I'm holding a Mimosa High reunion for everyone who ever went to the high school that we can find. It's going to be all day on the beach. We've located lots of former Mimosa Scorpions through the Internet and Facebook."

"Wow." A Mimosa High reunion. Could there be *anything* less appealing?

"And we're giving everyone a name tag with their senior adjective. Isn't a reunion an awesome way to spread the word about the resort and get people of all ages together?"

Amanda swallowed her response, because Lacey wouldn't understand that she'd been Mandy the Magnificent but would now be Mandy the Maid. "Awesome," she agreed.

"I'm sorry you have to work, but I'm desperate that day."

And the last thing she'd do was turn down triple time when she'd just groveled to get her job back. The only thing that mattered was accruing the money and sending it to Zeke Nicholas. "It's fine, as long as you don't make me wear *my* senior adjective."

"What was it?" Lacey asked.

Amanda shook her head. "I forget." Even though they both knew that no one forgot their senior adjective.

"I'm sorry Zeke isn't still here to attend," she said quickly. "Because meeting him really did give me the idea." She eyed Amanda. "Any chance he'll be back?"

She remembered the baseball team—had thought about it a lot, as a matter of fact. But he'd find a new location for his minor-league plans. He hadn't disappeared in the middle of the night only to return to build a baseball stadium. She'd already practiced squashing all hopes of that.

"I really don't know," Amanda answered honestly. "He left before I could ask him." *Or tell him how I really felt.*

Lacey nodded, pushing back from her desk to end the meeting. Amanda stood right away. "Thank you so much, Lacey."

The other woman came around her desk and reached both arms out. "If it's any consolation," she said, giving Amanda an easy and warm embrace, "Clay and I broke up once, too. But he came back."

It was, in fact, no consolation at all.

Chapter Thirteen

The giant orange ball dipped over the cobalt waters of the Gulf, moments from melting into an aww-inducing puddle of gold. Barefoot Bay had never looked more glorious for the reunion that spanned class members from almost sixty years. They didn't have senior adjectives before the 1970s, so the oldest party guests were over sixty and making up the nicknames now, based on memories.

And those tables were definitely having the most fun, Amanda thought as she bussed another set of martini glasses and carried them to the open-air bar. Although, to be fair, Lacey's idea was a huge success, with two hundred people falling in love with Casa Blanca, many sharing pictures on social media sites that would surely increase the resort's visibility and bookings.

Everyone was having fun...except Amanda. She was doing what she'd done for the past week. Cleaning up other people's messes and wallowing in her own. She missed Zeke more every day and here? At the reunion, where he'd be a superstar and she'd be...

No, she wouldn't be. If she'd ever had a chance with him, she'd blown it by lying and hurting him. Sighing for the sixtieth time that hour, she glanced around, hating the tiny little tickle of hope that played with her heart, imagining he might...

Stop it, you moron! He's not coming back.

There weren't that many representatives from the class of 2002 in the crowd, though Amanda had run into a few people she remembered. No one commented on her lowly maid status—at least not to her face. Overall, the atmosphere was too festive, the music too upbeat, and the booze was flowing too freely for anyone to be mean.

"Until now," Amanda muttered under her breath, squinting across the beach to confirm that, yes, the bitch was back.

Alone and dressed in her usual too-short, too-tight, and too-much, Tori kicked off her shoes and sashayed onto the sand.

"What's Tori the Tiger doing here?" The question came from behind the bar, making Amanda turn to meet the gaze of another housekeeper, who was also doing double duty working the big event.

"Class of 2002," Amanda said. "I guess she has as much right as any former Mimosa High student to be here."

Still, Amanda glanced around for Lacey to see if there was any reaction to the arrival of the former employee. Lacey stood in a large group, her baby—dressed in Mimosa High red-and-white overalls—on her hip. With her husband, Clay, at her side, Lacey was surrounded by friends and guests, reveling in the success of her party and her ever-growing business. She had no need to be concerned about Tori.

So Amanda wouldn't worry, either. Instead, she

finished bussing the glasses and scooped up her empty tray, ready to go look for more to clean up. As she turned, she almost smacked into Tori.

Oh, man. Really? "Excuse me," she said, trying to sidestep Tori.

"Oh, hello, Mrs. Lockhart." Her smile was tight as she slid her gaze over Amanda's uniform. "Interesting outfit for the reunion. No designer polka dots anymore? Oh, that's right. Turns out your sugar daddy wasn't so sweet after all."

Irritation skittered over her skin, tightening every nerve. Amanda forced a fake smile, refusing to make a scene at this event. "I'm working," she said through gritted teeth.

Tori glared at her, her gray eyes turning into angry slits. "Not if I have anything to say about it."

"You have nothing to say about it," Amanda replied. "You did your work, you wrecked enough things for me, now get out of my way."

One eyebrow tipped up. "Wrecked things for *you*? We lost the outsourcing, and Jared dumped me."

Smart man. "Sorry to hear that."

"Are you? No doubt you'll be after him next."

"Actually…" Amanda had to bite back a laugh. "There's plenty of doubt. I'm not interested."

Tori leaned in close enough that Amanda caught a whiff of beer on her breath. "Does Lacey know? Does anyone else at Casa Blanca know? It wasn't hard to find out you're still married to Mr. Wanted By The Law."

"Mandy Mitchell!" They both turned at the exclamation, Tori inching back and Amanda almost dancing for the reprieve. A beautiful young woman with long black hair stepped forward, her dark eyes focused

155

on Amanda. "You don't remember me, do you?"

"I'm afraid...wait." Amanda took in every detail of the woman's striking, unforgettable and exotic looks, but couldn't remember her name.

"Frankie." The woman put her hand out. "Frankie Cardinale. I was a freshman when you were a senior, so you probably don't remember me."

The name was familiar, but she really couldn't place a memory. "I'm sorry, I don't."

"Well, I remember you," she said, nodding.

For a moment, Amanda froze, waiting to hear of some horrible mistreatment she'd done back in her glory days.

"Don't tell me, she kicked you off the cheerleading squad for being too pretty."

The woman looked at Tori like she had an extra head. "Not by a long shot. My locker was by yours, Mandy. Because of some mistake, I was the only freshman in that hall." She gave Amanda a slow smile. "You were the only senior who gave me the time of day during what was a really challenging year for me."

Tori let out a little snort of disbelief.

"Oh! I do remember you," Amanda said, returning the smile, seeing a scared, dark-haired little girl in her memory. She reached out a hand to Frankie. "And I'm glad you're here."

"Mandy's glad because it gives her more work to do," Tori said. "She's on staff at the resort. A *maid*."

Frankie nodded, her interest piqued. "Cool. I'm trying to meet people who work here because..." She let her voice fade as a low thumping filled the air and all around, people started looking up to the sky, a crowd-wide cheer of excitement rising.

Amanda turned to the sunset, which often elicited applause, but this was different. The sound walloped through the air, drawing her gaze to the helicopter that hovered directly overhead.

For one long moment, Amanda stared slack-jawed and suddenly filled with so much hope she could taste it. Was it possible that—

"Well, someone wants to make a grand entrance," Tori said wryly.

Yes, someone did. Amanda's traitorous heart leapt into her throat as she closed her eyes and let the thudding blades match her pulse. He was coming back for her!

She fought the urge to run out and wave him down, watching the chopper dip left and right, zooming over the crowed and getting a huge hoot of pleasure from everyone around. Lots of glasses were raised, and people clapped and hollered, the sound deadened by the blood rushing in Amanda's head.

Once again, the bird tipped to either side, turned and flew over the crowd as if…he was looking for someone. Looking for…*her*?

Stop it. Stop it, she ordered herself. She hated the slow heat that crawled over her, hated the expectation and thrill that clutched her heart and wouldn't let go.

Suddenly, the helicopter popped higher into the air and flew to the north.

"Is he leaving?" someone called out.

No, Zeke! Don't leave! Amanda squeezed the tray so tightly it could have cracked in her hands. It had to be him. Who else? He was—

"Looking for a place to land!" another voice announced.

"Who is it?" a couple others called out.

Amanda squinted into the setting sun to see Lacey and her group, but they all seemed as surprised as anyone. Lacey even covered the ears of her crying baby.

Even this far away, Amanda could feel the pulse of the wind as the chopper dropped down on a deserted section of the beach. As though drawn magnetically, the crowd turned, and many started walking toward the new arrival.

"Let's go see," Frankie said, putting her hand on Amanda's arm. "Don't you want to know who from Mimosa High can afford to take a helicopter to the party?"

She ignored Tori's gaze locked on her. Only one man could...

No. She refused to let this hope steal her very breath. But how could she not? How could she not wish and dream that he rode in for her?

Still carrying her tray, Amanda let Frankie lead her with the crowd, closer to the thumping drum of helicopter blades, the rhythm matching the voice in her head.

He'd come back for her. He'd come back to help her. He'd come back...

It was crazy, it was wrong, it was stupid. And it was impossible not to fantasize.

"Hey, you're shaking," Frankie said.

"Hey, you're dreaming," Tori added, on her other side.

Amanda refused to look at either one of them. The crowd gathered closer to the helicopter, fifteen rows thick, with Amanda at the back as the noise finally abated.

And then the door popped open, and Amanda lifted the tray, pressing it to her heart as if she could stop the insane pulse that shook her. It had to be him. It had to be—

A man in a cowboy hat.

She had to bite her lip to keep from letting the cry of disappointment escape her. *Stupid, stupid girl.*

"Would you look at that?" Frankie whispered under her breath. "Take me to your rodeo, cowboy."

Tori elbowed her. "Not who you were expecting, was it, Cinderella?"

She fought the overwhelming urge to smack the tray right over Tori's head.

"'Scuse me?" The cowboy stepped closer to the crowd, his long, lanky body moving with purpose. He took the hat off and shook out some dark hair, peering into the crowd.

Holy cow, she knew that guy. It was Elliott Becker, one of the Niners she'd met in Miami.

"Anyone here know a man named Frank Cardinale?"

Next to her, Frankie gasped. "What the *eff*?"

And suddenly, it was all clear. The name Cardinale was familiar because she'd heard it at the party—the owner of the land they wanted to purchase for the baseball team. No Prince Charming had blown in on his chopper to sweep her away. He'd stayed away from a woman who'd lied and hurt him so bad…and sent someone else to do his work.

That didn't stop her from peering around the crowd and the tall cowboy to see into the helicopter on the off chance…

No. Elliott had come alone.

The only thing worse than the disappointment that

crushed her chest was the fact that Tori was right there, witnessing Amanda's defeat.

"I'm looking for Frank Cardinale," Elliott called out.

Still staring at him, still wishing to God he was someone else, Amanda whispered to the woman next to her. "I think he wants to buy your land."

When she didn't answer, Amanda glanced to her left, but Frankie was gone. She turned, looking at the crowd behind her, but the other woman was darting away, headed in the other direction down the beach.

"Excuse me, miss." A man tapped Amanda's shoulder, and she whipped around, thinking...

Oh, she had to stop this right now. She smiled at the older man. "Yes?"

"Could you clean up our table over here? We had a martini spill."

Amanda had to remember why she was here, and it wasn't to entertain fairy tales that did not come true. "Of course."

One more time, Tori jabbed her. "Give 'em hell, Mrs. Lockhart. I got some drinking to do."

On an exhale that caught in her too-tight throat, Amanda turned from the scene and headed back to her tables. The senior citizens were definitely getting rowdy, and someone had clocked two glasses and spilled gin over the table.

She reached for her rag, but she'd left it at the bar...where Tori now stood. Damn it, she didn't want to go back there. She glanced around again, tapping her pocket and wishing a dishrag would magically appear.

"Here, hon," that same older man said, holding his hand out. "Use this."

She gave him a grateful smile and took the paper towel, opening it to—

See words. Words written on the paper towel. She blinked at them, not able to read anything but seeing dark ink that had bled into the soft paper. A slow, agonizing trickle of awareness tiptoed up her spine, stealing her breath and making her head light.

Using two fingers, she spread the paper.

...do agree to pay...

She dropped the tray on the sand with a thud.

...imaginary girlfriend...

She squeezed her eyes shut. Was this a trick of the fading light? Tori's idea of a joke?

...activities that require the removal of...

"Where did you get this?" she whispered, tearing her gaze from the paper towel to the man next to her.

Silently, he pointed over her shoulder. Very slowly, as if in a dream, she turned around, and there he was. His hands in his pockets, his linen shirt loose in the breeze, his smile as sweet and warm and stunning as the sunset behind him.

For the time it took her heart to stop then speed into overtime, they stared at each other.

Zeke took a few steps closer, his blue eyes intent...and on her. Everything around them fell away, the laughter, the music, the world. When he was right in front of her, he dipped down on one knee, and then she heard the collective gasp from people around them.

What was he doing? "Zeke..." His name came out in a croak.

Looking down, he reached for the tray she'd dropped and lifted it to her. Oh, God, what a fool she was. She'd thought—

161

And he placed a folded piece of paper on top of it.

Still on one knee, he hoisted the tray higher, the paper on it fluttering in the breeze.

"All this needs is your signature."

The look on Mandy's face was all Zeke needed to be absolutely certain he'd done the right thing.

Not contacting her for a week had been one of the hardest things he'd ever done. But those achy nights—and all the effort to get back here—were worth the pure happiness he could see in her eyes.

She reached for him, closing her fingers around his forearm and tugging him up to her with enough strength in her touch for him to know she wanted him right where he wanted to be…closer.

"Is that what I think it is?" she whispered.

He nodded, keeping his vow not to say a word until her signature was on the divorce decree he'd paid a lot of money to some of the lowest people on Hong Kong's food chain to get signed by her ex. It hadn't been that hard, based on what he was able to find out about Doug Lockhart. Not hard for a man like Zeke, who had connections all over the world.

Information and location and access were all easily bought with a few million dollars.

The job had been expensive, yes. But he'd have paid six times that much if he'd had to. Ten. A hundred. Whatever it took for this moment and Mandy to be his.

As he stood, she held his gaze, a gorgeous glisten in

her green eyes, the tears the kind he'd hoped she'd shed.

"How?" she asked.

He angled his head as if to say, *Do you really need to ask?* Next to him, Paul Jameson, one of Zeke's longtime top managers, produced a pen.

"I will witness and notarize the second signature," Paul said.

"The second..." Mandy looked from one to the other, letting out a soft laugh. "You *are* relentless."

Zeke didn't answer, but Paul nodded to the document. "Go ahead, ma'am," Jameson said. "It is one hundred percent official."

Her hands trembled as she opened the paper and then let out an audible sigh as she read the words Zeke had memorized already.

Final decree of dissolution of marriage.

Paul had only included the last page, the important one that required her signature. Right next to Douglas B. Lockhart's. B for bastard.

The bastard who was already in the hands of federal authorities. But not, Zeke had made sure, until he'd signed his divorce decree.

Once again, Mandy looked up at him. "Thank you."

He mouthed one word. "Sign."

Without hesitation, she put the pen to the paper and scribbled her name. Still looking down, she set the pen on the tray and took a slow, deep breath.

"That doesn't make anything legal." Tori muscled her way closer, her face pink with anger and jealousy. "She's still married!"

Taking the signed paper, Zeke turned and shoved the tray into Tori's hands. "Would you mind? And while you're at it..." He sneaked a wink at Mandy before adding, "Get some class, Tori, because you obviously have none."

Her jaw unhinged, but Paul nudged the woman away, so Zeke could return his attention to Mandy, who still looked bewildered...and beautiful. She reached her hands up to his face, putting her warm fingers on his cheeks.

"I can only guess how, but...why?"

She didn't know why? "Because I..." *Love you.* "I want you to be happy." Which were one and the same, weren't they? He would make her happy...forever.

"I am," she admitted. "Happier than you can imagine. I saw the helicopter, and I thought..." She blinked a tear. "I hoped you'd be on it."

"As if I'd be that much of a cliché. I leave the grand gestures to Becker. Paul and I drove in a few minutes ago."

She stifled a half-laugh, half-cry. "I really wanted you to come back to me." Her voice cracked, and that did such stupid things to his heart.

"You doubted that I would?" How could she?

"Of course. I lied to you. I hurt you. You disappeared in the middle of the night."

"I had work to do, Mandy. Work to make it completely right for us to be together." He wrapped his arms around her and pulled her into him to whisper in her ear. "I never considered for one second that I wouldn't come back to you. But I wasn't going to say another word until you were—*are*—a free woman."

"I am free." A soft shudder ran through her. "That's all I've wanted. Not independence, freedom...to love. There's a difference, isn't there?"

"Huge," he agreed, stroking her hair as he held her close. "As long as you love me, you can have all the freedom you want and need."

She inched back, her eyes darkening. He couldn't breathe as he watched emotions play over her face and realization settle on her heart. "I could," she sighed. "I could love you."

"What's this 'could' business?" Without a second's hesitation, he reached down and scooped her into his arms, getting a small shriek of surprise as he cradled her. A crowd had circled them, cheering and clapping.

"Zeke!" she exclaimed, wrapping her arms around his neck. He hoisted her higher and started across the sand. "What are you doing?"

"What I should have done in high school," he said loudly. The crowd parted as he powered through, the sound of her laughter and cries of joy almost drowned out by the cheering and the thump of the chopper blades as they started up. "Watch out, world. Ezekiel the Geekiel got the best girl of all!"

A few familiar faces came into his view, blurred like they were in high school, except for the one that had never been anything but crystal clear. The face of the woman he loved, holding on for her life.

Mandy laughed as he lifted her into the helicopter, and they both turned and waved at the crowd.

"I can't believe you did that!" she said, breathless. "Oh, look!" She lifted her left hand, holding a balled paper towel. "I still have our contract."

He snagged the paper, holding a corner so the document that brought them together fluttered like a dragonfly in the wind. "We don't need any contracts except the one that says forever and ever." He leaned over to kiss her. "And clothing optional."

The paper sailed off over the Gulf of Mexico,

floating on their love and laughter.

He yanked the door closed and pulled her into him. "Buckle up for the ride of a lifetime, Mandy Mitchell."

"Is that my name again?"

"Not for long."

Want to kick off your shoes and fall in love again? Elliott Becker's story picks up where this one left off…and another unforgettable hero is about to be swept off his feet in Barefoot Bay.

Excerpt from

Seduction on the Sand

The Barefoot Bay Series #2

Roxanne St. Claire

Chapter One

Elliott Becker climbed out of the helicopter and strode across the beach without bothering to apologize for his dramatic arrival that unexpectedly halted a high school reunion. A lot of faces in the crowd stared back at him, all easy to read. Men narrowed their eyes in distrust because he was wearing a Stetson and arrived by chopper. Women ogled openly because, well, he was wearing a Stetson and arrived by chopper.

He cleared his throat, tipped his hat back, and applauded himself for choosing this reunion to start his search. His goal had nothing to do with Mimosa High, but this was an easy way to reach a lot of island residents at one time. And *easy* was the only way he rolled.

"I'm looking for a man named Frank Cardinale," he announced to the crowd that had gathered when his helicopter had landed on the sand.

From under the rim of his hat, he scanned the crowd, catching a quick movement in the back. Long dark hair fluttered as a woman darted away, moving with just enough purpose that her retreat couldn't have been coincidental.

No one answered his question right away, so he zeroed in on the lady who'd left. With some luck, she'd lead him right to Mr. Cardinale. And if there was one thing Elliott Becker had a ton of, it was luck. And money. And charm. And some damn fine looks. He was about to put all of them to good use.

He followed his instinct and the sway of wavy waist-length hair the color of coffee beans. In a sheer cotton skirt that clung to her hips and danced around her ankles, she made an easy, and lovely, mark.

She power-walked down the beach, away from the resort and the party, heading straight to the frothy white shore where the Gulf of Mexico swirled in low tide. Just as her bare feet reached the water line, she glanced over her shoulder, too quickly for him to get a look at her face. But he could easily see her narrow shoulders tighten and her long legs pick up speed.

Interesting. Maybe someone didn't *want* him to find the owner of the twenty acres in Barefoot Bay that he and his partners needed to close this deal. The plans to build a small baseball stadium and start a minor-league team on Mimosa Key were supposed to be secret, but he and his partners had already nailed down verbals on three plots in the northeast corner of the island. Word could have gotten out that they wanted that last twenty acres, even though the other landowners had signed nondisclosures. On an island less than ten miles long and three miles wide? Even scads of money didn't buy silence.

He matched her quickened steps. No, she wasn't out for a sunset stroll; she was running. Not literally. Not yet, anyway. But definitely moving away from Elliott for a reason. A reason he had every intention of finding out.

It didn't take more than a few long strides to catch up, but he stayed about a foot behind her.

"I bet you know where I can find Frank Cardinale," he said, keeping his voice low and unthreatening.

She didn't turn, pretending not to hear him.

"Otherwise, why would you take off like a twister in a trailer park?"

That slowed her step. In fact, it stopped her completely. Elliott felt his mouth turn up in a satisfied grin. The Texas drawl always got 'em. Of all the moves his military family had made, he'd lived in the Lone Star State for only a year, but it was enough to pick up a few expressions and work on the twang. And, hell, he looked excellent in a cowboy hat. Now if she'd only turn—

"I live in a trailer." Her words were nearly lost with the splash of a wave at her feet.

Shoot. Way to blow the first impression. "It's just a turn of phrase, ma'am."

"More like an expression of condescension and mockery."

"No, a way to say you're moving too fast, not an insult to your home." He took two more steps, close enough to notice how the late afternoon light made her skin glow and pick up a whiff of something flowery and pretty. "After all, home is where the heart is," he said. Not that he'd know, but he'd certainly heard that enough in his life.

"It's not for sale." She spun around, making her hair swing like a curtain opening to a stage play. "So get back on your fancy helo, cowboy, and leave me alone."

He blinked at her, still not fully processing the demand because, man, oh, man, she was pretty. No, she rounded pretty and slid right into gorgeous, despite the fire in whiskey-gold eyes and the daring set of a delicate jaw.

"What are you staring at?" she demanded. "Are you deaf or just dumb as dirt?"

"Blind. By your beauty."

"Oh, *puh*lease." She looked skyward and sighed. "Spare me the lines."

"That's not a line."

Her eyes turned into golden slits of sheer disbelief.

"Okay, it's a line," he conceded. "But in this case, it's also true."

"Did you hear me? It's not for sale."

Yeah, he'd heard her, and the statement was starting to make sense, considering he'd come to the barrier island for one purpose, and it wasn't to flirt with sexy brunettes on the beach. Not that he'd fight the inevitable, but his goal was to buy land, and these words were not what he wanted to hear, no matter how scrumptious the mouth that spoke them.

"Do you know Frank Cardinale?" he asked.

She crossed her arms, which was patently unfair considering what that did to her cleavage. "I *am* Frank Cardinale."

He snorted softly and didn't fight the need to examine her breasts further. 'Cause, hell, now he had an excuse. "Considering ol' Frank is in his eighties and a man, I'd say you have one hell of a plastic surgeon, Mr. C."

"Miss," she corrected. "Miss Francesca Cardinale." She squeezed her upper arms as if nature and good manners were telling her to reach out and offer a handshake but she had to ignore the order. "Frank was my grandfather. He's dead."

The lady wasn't married, and the landowner was dead.

Meaning this little excursion to the remote island would be fast, easy and possibly quite fun. He refused to smile at the thought, but took off his hat with one hand and extended the other. "I'm very sorry for your loss. I'm Elliott Becker."

She didn't take his hand, but met his gaze. "I know why you're here. You're not the first person to come sniffing around the land. Although you're the first to drop down like you owned the place."

"Which I don't." But he intended to.

The thump of helicopter blades pulled his attention. There went Zeke, whisking away the woman he'd recently gone stupid in love over. Zeke had taken the chopper for the day, leaving Elliott with the task of finding Frank—er, *Francesca*—Cardinale to close the land deal.

"But you're not getting my land, Mr. Becker, so you better find another ride out of Barefoot Bay." She gave him a tight smile, which only made him want to see that pretty face lit up with real happiness.

"Maybe you could give me one."

"A ride? Maybe not." She took off, not even bothering to end the conversation.

"I can walk with you, then."

"No."

He fell in step with her anyway. "Can I call you Francesca?"

"Make that a hell no." She refused to look at him.

He kept stride. "So, what's your price?"

That got him a quick look and almost—*almost*—a smile of admiration. Of course. Women loved relentless men. In cowboy hats. With Texas twangs.

"My price is too high for you."

And money. Women *loved* money, and he had even

more of that than charm and sex appeal. "Not to be, you know, immodest or anything, but cash really isn't an issue."

She stopped and closed her eyes, so close to a smile he could almost taste it. And, damn, he wanted to. "Good for you, but let me make this clear: I don't want to talk to you, walk with you, or sell you one blade of grass that I own." With that, she powered on, shoulders square, head high, bare feet kicking up little wakes of sand and sea.

Damn, those were pretty feet. Would be even prettier if they weren't moving so fast in the wrong direction.

"Course there is the fact that you don't, uh, actually *own* that land." He cleared his throat. "Unless you really are Frank Cardinale."

Her speed wavered, her shoulders slumped, and she let her head drop in resignation. "What do I have to do to make you go away?"

"Smile."

She slowly turned to him. "Excuse me?"

"Smile for me."

She did, like a kid being forced to say cheese.

"A real smile." He gave her a slow, easy one of his own, lopsided and genuine enough to melt hearts and weaken knees and remove any clothing that needed to go. "Like this."

For a second, he might have had her. He saw the flicker of female response, the ever so slight darkening of her eyes, the thump of a pulse at the base of her throat. "The property is not for sale, and please don't bother taking this conversation one step further because the answer will be an unmistakable, unequivocal, indisputable no."

"A hundred thousand?"

She practically choked. "What part of that didn't you understand?"

"The long, unspellable words might throw me, but I got the 'no' loud and clear." He winked. "A million?"

Very slowly, she shook her head.

Oh, for cryin' out loud, let's get this done. "Five million? Ten? Fifteen? Everyone has a price, Francesca."

Then her face relaxed and her lips curled up and her eyes lit with something that reached right down into his gut and sucker punched him. "Not for a billion. Which I doubt you have."

She started to walk away again, and he lost the fight not to touch her. Reaching out, he closed his hand over her elbow and stopped her, pulling her very gently toward him so he could turn over his trump card, low and sweet and right in her ear.

"I have two billion. And a half, to be precise. I'm willing to part with enough to buy your land, make you a rich woman, and celebrate over dinner together. Do we have a deal?"

A glimmer of amusement lit her eyes, as gold as the sunset behind her now. "Is everything this easy for you?"

He laughed softly, mostly at the truth of that statement. "Just about."

"Was it easy to become a billionaire?"

Disgustingly so. He went for a self-effacing shrug. "Mostly a mix of good timing, dumb luck, and my irresistible boyish charm."

"Really?" One beautifully arched eyebrow lifted toward the sky. "Well, guess what, Elliott Becker?" She cooed his name, already softening. The *B* in billion usually did that when his world-class flirting missed the mark. "Your luck ran out, your timing sucks, and I don't find you charming, boyish, or the least bit irresistible."

Undaunted, he took a step closer and lifted his hand, grazing her chin. "Bet I can change your mind."

"Bet you can't." She pivoted and took off so fast, she kicked a clump of sand on his jeans.

Brushing it, he just grinned. "How much are you willing to bet?" he called out. "I put fifteen million on the table!"

She stuck up her middle finger and kept running.

Sweet.

The only thing Becker liked more than a sexy woman with attitude was a sexy woman with attitude *and* a piece of real estate he wanted. This could be a good time. Maybe not quite as easy as he'd thought, but sometimes *hard* could be fun, too.

Don't Miss a Moment in Barefoot Bay!

Don't miss Roxanne St. Claire's latest popular series, The Dogfather, which is chock full of hot guys, cute dogs, true love…and one great big Irish family you will adore!

Daniel Kilcannon is known as "The Dogfather" for a reason. It's not just his renowned skills as a veterinarian, his tremendous love of dogs, or the fact that he has turned his homestead in the foothills of the Blue Ridge Mountains into a world class dog training and rescue facility. Ask his six grown children who run Waterford Farm for him, and they'll tell you that their father's nickname is due to his uncanny ability to pull a few strings to get what he wants. And what he wants is for his four sons and two daughters to find the kind of life-changing love he had with his dearly departed wife, Annie. This old dog has a few new tricks…and he'll use them all to see his pack all settled into their happily ever afters!

Every book in the Dogfather series features a rescue dog on the cover and a portion of proceeds are donated to the Alaqua Animal Refuge, where the covers were photographed. And every story has a dog at the heart of the romance…front, center, and sometimes right in between. If you love dogs and romance, this series is for you!

The Dogfather Series

Turn the page for a sneak peek of Sit…Stay…Beg.

Sit...Stay...Beg

The Dogfather Series – Book One

Daniel Kilcannon opened his eyes on the morning after he buried his wife of thirty-six years and pushed himself up, not creaking too badly for fifty-six years young. His movement instantly woke Rusty, sprawled at the foot of the bed. The Irish setter lifted his glossy red head, a little hope in his big brown eyes as if to ask, *Is she back yet?*

"Bad news, my boy. It's still just you and me."

He dragged his hands through his thick hair, the next wave of grief bearing down, growing all too familiar since the moment his beloved wife succumbed to a heart attack in the prime of her life. When the wave passed, he tried to think clearly. About today. Beyond today.

What could possibly matter now that Annie was gone?

The kids.

Of course, Daniel and Annie Kilcannon had been driven by one thing as a couple: to do what was best for their children, no matter how old the six of them were. And the way they were living now?

Not *best* for his far-flung six-pack.

Annie used to say, *You're only as happy as your least-happy kid.*

And today, none of them could be called happy, and not just because they'd had to say goodbye to a mother they loved with their whole hearts and souls.

Not one of them, with the possible exception of Aidan, was fully content. Three of them had picked up and moved across the country to the Pacific Northwest to follow their brother Garrett when he sold his company. Now they all worked for an industry behemoth, and it wasn't fun like it was when they were helping Garrett run a start-up in Chapel Hill. Liam openly loathed the Seattle hipsters, didn't even *drink* coffee, and was broodier than ever, if that was possible. And Shane was a damn good attorney, but he didn't seem to have any enthusiasm for the meaningless corporate contracts he'd been stuck with out there.

Darcy's wanderlust was rearing its capricious head again, making her threaten to quit her job and head to Australia or Austria—he couldn't remember which—to catch up with her wayward cousin and get into whatever trouble those two always were getting into.

And Garrett? He'd been on fire when he started that Internet company a few years ago. The most restless of Daniel's six kids, Garrett had found his passion and thrived in a world that combined his technological prowess and leadership skills. But then Garrett chased the almighty dollar and gave up control. Sure, he'd made them all a pile of money, but it cost the boy his soul, because ever since he signed that contract and sold his company a month ago, he'd changed. It was like he'd built a wall around himself, and nothing could take it down.

Molly stayed right here in Bitter Bark and had taken over Daniel's veterinary practice in town. But even with the special relationship she enjoyed with her daughter, Molly had a sadness in her eyes, too, since most of her siblings had moved across the country.

They all needed to be home and be a family, now more than ever. And they needed families of their own.

And, clearly, they needed a little help to make that happen.

Oh hell, they didn't call him the Dogfather just because he was a damn good vet who'd rescued and raised a lot of dogs in his time. He could still hear Annie's wind-chime laugh and tender touch as she teased him with the nickname that suited both his love of animals and his ability to get people to do what he wanted.

Except, he hadn't been able to get Annie to live. He swallowed at the sharp pain in his chest, fighting the sting of tears. He had to manage the grief and agony and emptiness. And he would, because Annie wouldn't want him moping around like a basset hound without a bone.

"I have to make them realize how much happier they'd be back home in Bitter Bark, North Carolina," he said to his dog, who'd jumped off the bed and rubbed his head against Daniel's leg.

The dog barked once, which Daniel took as a hearty agreement, but was probably a reminder that it was time for Rusty to visit the grass.

"I'm not *manipulating* them," he said, feeling the need to defend the idea that was taking hold. He was being a fifty-six-year-old widower who wanted his family whole and happy.

On a sigh, he wandered to the window, pushed back the sheer curtain, and looked out over what he could see of the nearly one hundred acres of Waterford Farm. His gaze drifted over the rolling hills, the woods laden with the golds and reds of fall, the sunshine glistening like crystals on the pond.

Closer to the main house, which had grown and been remodeled repeatedly over the last thirty years, he could see Liam and Shane in the pen outside the kennels, already working with the two foster Dobies Annie had taken in before she died.

Garrett was perched on a split-rail fence, watching his brothers snap their fingers and dole out treats and affection to get the new rescues to obey. Garrett turned toward the house, and after a few seconds, Molly and Aidan came into sight, side by side, next in line in age, carrying coffee mugs, deep in conversation.

What a shame that Aidan's first chance to come home as an Army Ranger was for his mother's funeral. Behind them, Darcy came bounding out, her fluffball of a Shih Tzu, aptly named Kookie, on her heels.

Leaning against the glass, he watched the scene unfold, aching for his wife. Annie would love this, standing together in the bedroom window, spying on their now-grown offspring as they played with the dogs, both of them drowning in pride and love for this strong, solid, smart brood of theirs.

A gentle tap on his door pulled his attention, and since he could see all six of his kids and knew for certain his nine-year-old granddaughter was still asleep, that left only one person who'd spent the night after the funeral in his big, empty home. "Come in, Gramma Finnie."

The door inched open to his eighty-three-year-old mother, already dressed in a crisp cotton blouse and brightly colored cardigan, her short white hair styled, her pink lipstick and rouge applied with care. "Just checking on you, lad."

He was so not a *lad* anymore, but his mother, who'd lived in Ireland until she was twenty, still had a lilting brogue and still thought of all males under eighty as *lads*.

"I'm watching the kids in the yard," he said, beckoning her to join him.

"They're hardly kids."

"To me, they are."

With a soft laugh, she came closer, adjusting her wire-rimmed bifocals to get a good look. "It's what Seamus always wanted," she said wistfully, smiling as she did any time she spoke of her husband, Daniel's father, gone ten years now. "The day we arrived from Ireland and stepped foot on this land in 1954, he wanted two things for this homestead."

Kids and dogs.

Daniel had heard the story a thousand times but humored his mother, his heart too bruised from the reminder that life was far too short to interrupt a natural storyteller like Finola Kilcannon.

"'Finnie,' he said. 'We've got a lot of money and a lot of land. Let's name this place after the company that made us rich and fill it with the things we love most: kids and dogs.'"

Of course, he knew Waterford Farm was named after the famed Irish company that bought the glassblowing business Seamus had inherited from his father. Made wealthy enough to leave Ireland by the deal, twenty-five-year-old Seamus Kilcannon had taken his wife and baby son to America in search of land and a new life.

"And we did our best," she continued. "Three kids, though…" She tipped her head, the mention of his older brother, Liam, still, after all these years, painful for her. "And more dogs rescued, raised, or fostered than I can count." She looked up at him, her crystal-blue eyes watery. "But it wasn't until you and Annie got married that his dream was truly fulfilled."

Married in a big fat hurry, he thought, thanks to the unexpected conception of his eldest son. With Daniel still in veterinarian school and a baby on the way, the young couple had moved into Waterford Farm at the urging of Seamus and Finola, a couple who'd had their own unexpected conception of a son, also named Liam.

Then along came Shane, and when Annie was pregnant with Garrett, his parents decided to move to an old Victorian home in town and hand over all the land and the house to the growing second generation of American Kilcannons. And, of course, Daniel and Annie continued the tradition of taking in dogs, training and housing them in a small five-stall kennel that Daniel and his older sons built with their own hands.

"And now those kids are all moved on," he said, hating the broken sound of his voice.

"They're right there," his mother said. "Where they belong."

"They do belong here," he said, returning to the thought that had woken him this morning. "They're all happiest here."

"Then keep them here, lad."

"How can I do that without interfering in their lives?"

"Give them a choice and see what they choose. They know their own hearts."

Daniel thought about that, an idea—a fantasy, really—taking shape.

"You know that Annie and I drew up plans to expand the barn and shelter, add training areas and classrooms, and build Waterford Farm into a top-notch dog rescue, training, shelter, and veterinary business."

"And now those plans are dead?" she asked.

No, Annie was dead. He leaned his head against the

cool glass and gave in to a sigh that made Rusty come and check on his master.

"I know, I know," he muttered. "I have to think about it."

His mother stepped back from the window. "You're in mournin', lad. But you know you'll never plow a field by turning it over in your mind," she said, an Irish proverb always at the ready.

And always right.

Suddenly, Molly turned and looked up at the window, spying him there. She tilted her head to the side, her chocolate-colored curls falling over drooping shoulders, her expression as easy to read as one of the puppies'.

Are you all right, Dad?

He saw her say something to Aidan, who looked up, and that same sympathy changed the young warrior's face to something softer. Liam and Shane stopped training the dogs to gaze up, too, their muscular bodies tightening with the hit of pain. He could read Garrett's lips as he dragged his hand through his thick, dark hair and muttered, "Poor Dad."

After a moment, Darcy reached both arms up toward the window and flicked her fingers, inviting him to join them, the same sadness in her expression.

His mother put a hand on his shoulder, pulling his attention to her weathered face. "Giving this homestead and all the land to you while we were still alive was the easiest decision Seamus and I ever made. Maybe it's time you ask your children if they'd like the same thing."

He knew she was right.

She leaned over and ruffled Rusty's fur. "You think

about that, and I'll take this darlin' boy out to the yard."
She started to go out, and Rusty didn't hesitate to follow.
"That's a good dog," she whispered. "You know I've got
a weakness for ya, puppy. You're the spittin' image of
my Corky. Did I tell you about Corky? He was with us
on that September day in the year of our Lord nineteen
hundred and fifty-four when we drove that old bucket o'
bolts into the town of Bitter Bark, and when Seamus
read the sign, that dog made so much noise that…"

Her brogue faded along with Rusty's footsteps on the
hardwood of the hall, leaving Daniel completely alone to
gaze at his family out the window.

You're only as happy as your least-happy kid.

It was time to fix that. And if they all came back to
where they belonged, maybe he could help each of them
find a love as strong and real as the one he and Annie
had shared. Not interfere, no. Just guide them, as he
always had.

The decision made, his heart felt lighter.

He turned to the big empty bed where he'd shared so
many laughs, so much love, and thirty-six deeply content
years with Annie.

He could imagine her loving smile. Feel her hand on
his shoulder. Sense her spirit next to him. And, Lord, he
could hear her sweet, sensible, stable voice.

*Go, Daniel. Be the Dogfather and make them an offer
they can't refuse.*

More Books by Roxanne St. Claire

Prior to writing the Barefoot Bay series, Roxanne wrote romantic suspense in two popular series, and several stand alones. All titles are still available in digital versions and many are available in print.

THE GUARDIAN ANGELINOS (ROMANTIC SUSPENSE)
Edge of Sight
Shiver of Fear
Face of Danger

THE BULLET CATCHERS (ROMANTIC SUSPENSE)
Kill Me Twice
Thrill Me to Death
Take Me Tonight
First You Run
Then You Hide
Now You Die
Hunt Her Down
Make Her Pay
Pick Your Poison (a novella)

STAND-ALONE NOVELS (ROMANCE AND SUSPENSE)
Space in His Heart
Hit Reply
Tropical Getaway
French Twist
Killer Curves
Don't You Wish (Young Adult)

About The Author

Published since 2003, Roxanne St. Claire is a *New York Times* and *USA Today* bestselling author of more than fifty romance and suspense novels.

In addition to being an ten-time nominee and one-time winner of the prestigious RITA™ Award for the best in romance writing, Roxanne's novels have won the National Readers' Choice Award for best romantic suspense four times, as well as the Maggie, the Daphne du Maurier Award, the HOLT Medallion, Booksellers' Best, Book Buyers Best, the Award of Excellence, and many others.

A recent empty-nester, she lives in Florida with her husband, and still attempts to run the lives of her young adult children. She loves dogs, books, chocolate, and wine, especially all at the same time!

www.roxannestclaire.com
www.twitter.com/roxannestclaire
www.facebook.com/roxannestclaire
www.instagram.com/roxannestclaire1

Made in the USA
Columbia, SC
20 March 2019